Bullseye Breach

ANATOMY OF AN ELECTRONIC BREAK-IN

Greg Scott

BULLSEYE BREACH: ANATOMY OF AN ELECTRONIC BREAK-IN
Copyright © 2015 by Greg Scott

All rights reserved. No part of this book may be reproduced by any mechanical, photographic, or electronic process, or in the form of a phonographic recording, nor may it be stored in a retrieval system, transmitted, or otherwise be copied for public or private use, other than for "fair use" as brief quotations embodied in articles and reviews without prior written permission of the publisher.

This is a work of fiction. The people, corporations, organizations, institutions, circumstances, and events depicted are fictitious and a product of the author's imagination. Any resemblance of any character to any actual person, either living or dead, is purely coincidental.

ISBN 13: 978-1-59298-877-8

Library of Congress Catalog Number: 2015903779

Printed in the United States of America

First Printing: 2015

19 18 17 16 15 5 4 3 2 1

Edited by Steve LeBeau, Lily Coyle, and Alicia Ester
Cover and interior design by Laura Drew.
Cover photography © shutterstock.

Beaver's Pond Press
7108 Ohms Lane
Edina, MN 55439–2129
952-829-8818
www.beaverspondpress.com

www.bullseyebreach.com
www.infrasupport.com

Dedicated to the unsung heroes on the front lines in bank fraud departments across the United States; especially to Kim, with the real-world US Bank Fraud Department, who saved my butt when she helped me track down at least $14,773.92 in attempted fraudulent transactions on my own credit card on December 1, 2011.

And to the IT security professionals in the trenches who work hard to keep us safe on the Internet. May everyone who reads this book heed their warnings.

Table of Contents

Why Yet Another Book on IT Security?	1
Cybercrime Seminar	4
Rousseau Plumbing and Mechanical	18
Ivan Tarski	26
Dark Secrets	37
Hacking the Hacker	40
Bangalore	51
More Reconnaissance	53
Three FTP Sites	59
The Russians Need a New Approach	63
Bullseye Office	64
One Step Closer	71
Danger	73
Manipulating the Mob	85
Final Preparations	89
The Spigot Opens	93
Tenderloin	96
Den of Thieves	100
First Alerts	109
Regina	118
Jerry Barkley	136
Getting Organized	145

Operation Lemonade	172
Power of the Press	180
Shutting Down the Pipeline	186
Lemonade & Vodka Coolers	196
Trouble in Russia	197
Full Circle	202
January Golf	206
The Boardroom	209
Acknowledgments	230

Prologue
Why Yet Another Book on IT Security?

Several years ago, I visited a potential customer and showed her how her business was vulnerable to cyberattacks. But I made a mistake—I used a computer and computer screens to illustrate the threats she faced. It was a short meeting. As I tried to explain subjects such as malware and phishing and open TCP ports and IP addresses and NAT, and the threats she faced, she told me she already had somebody who could reset passwords and showed me the door.

Another time, I met with an executive at a bank who also wanted me to go away. In an effort to show he already had all the security he needed, he confidently handed me a folder with the results from a security study he paid somebody else to do. I looked over the report, and then said, "This looks good. They did a good job describing the issues around your website. Where's the part about your internal network right here at the bank?"

His reply was quick. "Thanks for coming by. There's the door and have a nice day."

Another time, I ran a virus scan on the store computer at a small retailer and found hundreds of compromised files. When I tried explaining that sharing her public Wi-Fi service with her private store network was like walking into a closed room full of contagious people, she called her bookkeeper and decided it wasn't worth her time or money to fix it. It was another short meeting.

I've seen countless scenarios play out in hundreds of organizations over the years and they all have one common attribute—a decision maker either unable or unwilling to believe IT security issues are relevant.

And after all these years, maybe I finally get it. IT concepts are abstract and business decision makers don't deal in the abstract. They deal in the here and now. Security practitioners need to adjust how we present this stuff.

So this book tells a fictional story, inspired by recent headlines, about a large scale attack. You'll meet some bad guys, the clueless, a few victims, and some good guys who come up with a creative way to fight back.

Take away three real-world lessons:

1. You're right; you probably don't have any secrets anyone cares about. But you're not the target; you're part of the path to the target. Maybe somebody fooled you into running the wrong program and now he or she wants you to pay a ransom to unscramble all your company documents. Or maybe somebody is using you to steal somebody else's secrets. Either way, the fallout will be bad for your business. Just ask Max Rousseau. Or Frank Wright. Or even better, Frank's son.

2. The Internet criminal industry is well funded, resourceful, and smart. The bad guys have an entire value chain, including raw material suppliers, manufacturers, logistics, and end user customers. It's an arms race and the good guys are outnumbered and outgunned.

3. Your security practices have real-world consequences, some of them far beyond your company walls. Read about Regina Lopez, who represents millions of real-world innocent victims ensnared by the poor security practices of one large retailer.

Prologue

The threats are real and the scenarios presented in this book are adapted from real life. Don't bury your head in the sand and pretend your IT systems are not important just because you don't understand them. The Internet is here to stay and you need to protect the confidentiality, integrity, and availability of your data. The future of your company depends on it.

I hope you enjoy reading this story as much as I enjoyed getting to know the characters and writing it.

One more note to keep me out of hot water: although inspired by real life events, the story in this book is straight out of my imagination. It's fiction. I made it up.

Cybercrime Seminar

"ALL WARFARE IS BASED ON DECEPTION."
SUN TZU, CHINESE STRATEGIST (544 BC-496 BC)

Beneath every inch of the Internet superhighway is a vast sewer system, the underground home of cybercriminals who...

Jerry Barkley abruptly paused in the middle of his speech on cybercrime, because he suddenly realized he was the only man in the room not wearing a suit. He gazed across the audience at the Retail Council monthly luncheon tucked in a second floor conference room in the Minneapolis Convention Center. These executives and their staffs represented the entire gamut of retail stores in Minneapolis, from Fortune 500 companies to small businesses. Some wore custom-tailored Italian silks, some wore off-the-rack polyester, but they all wore suits. Jerry didn't feel inferior as much as he just felt out of place. Most of his friends were people in low places, regular folks who valued him for his independent spirit and practical knowledge of computers and networking. They didn't care that he wore tennis shoes and slightly faded khakis. Besides, for this lunchtime talk he wore his very best sweater, the one with all the swirly colors that reminded him of modern art. As far as Jerry was concerned, he was plenty dressed up for the occasion.

There were just a few women in the room, and most of them wore suits or businesslike dresses. Wait—there was a cute brunette wearing blue jeans back at the Bullseye Corp. table. Jerry didn't realize he had broken into a big grin when he saw her, but when she smiled back and their eyes met, the shock quickly brought him to his senses.

"—Uhh, so these cybercriminals could be anywhere in the world with an Internet connection, and while you're sleeping, they're wide awake and thinking of new ways to rip you off. I cannot emphasize enough the importance of standing guard against credit-card fraud…"

This last comment caught the attention of Bullseye CEO Daniel Berger, who was wearing a splendid blue suit from London that probably cost more than Jerry's car. Bullseye was a giant among big-box discount retailers, with over 2,000 stores in the US and Canada. Berger leaned over and whispered to his chief information officer sitting next to him, Liz Isaacs.

"Liz, do we have a credit-card problem?"

"Hardly," she replied. "It's negligible and decreasing each year. Our biggest crimes are shoplifting and employee theft."

"That's what I thought. So why am I here listening to this? What I'm really interested in is the spring shopping forecast."

But Berger knew exactly why he had to be there—because the Bullseye board of directors wanted him there. Mostly at the insistence of one director in particular, Henri Carpentier, who was on a security kick. Carpentier also sat on the board of a multinational bank, so he heard plenty of scare stories. And he liked to retell one of his own stories from his days as chief operating officer at digital media conglomerate WooHoo, Inc. about an Alaskan politician. Berger was tired of hearing it.

Ordinarily Berger would have fought coming to something like this, but he was already in the doghouse because of the company's performance. For one thing, the Canadian store rollout was a nightmare. There were problems with construction, zoning, operations, sales, pricing—everything. When he soft-pedaled the situation at the last board meeting by saying the Canadian stores were "performing slightly below expectations," the other board members rolled their eyes. The US-store quarterly numbers were also troubling, and that was after a subpar 2012 holiday season. Berger was counting on record 2013 holiday sales to save his butt. Credit-card fraud? The only security he needed was his own job security.

"...And of course the concept of the Trojan horse goes back to ancient Greece, where the Athenian army tricked the people of Troy by offering them a large wooden horse as a token of their surrender. The Athenians pretended to sail away, so the Trojans rolled the giant horse into the city, proud of the gift that honored their victory. But hidden inside that wooden statue were Athenian soldiers. When night fell they crawled out of the horse, opened the gates of the city, and let in the Athenian army to conquer Troy at last.

"Today's clever cybercriminals also use trickery. If you see an email with an attachment you can open for a screensaver or maybe a link for free Viagra, don't open it. It probably has a little program buried inside that will sit dormant for a while until it unleashes its payload. That's why I always warn my customers to 'Beware of geeks bearing gifts.'"

Jerry stopped for a second to let the laughter roll in, but it didn't. There were scattered groans around the room but most people sat expressionless. A few smiled politely, but the only audible chuckle came from the Bullseye table. "At least that lady in the blue jeans got a kick out of it," thought Jerry. "What's wrong with these people?"

Berger leaned over to Liz again and asked, "What do you think of this guy?"

"Well," said Liz, "how can you take him seriously? He's wearing tennis shoes!"

Liz Isaacs was impeccably dressed in an Armani muted-gray cashmere blazer, an ivory blouse by Gucci, and a vintage Dior plaid skirt. She had been dressing for success since grade school. Nearly six feet tall and strikingly pretty with brown hair down to her chin, Liz could have been a model, but she wanted a CEO's corner office some day and all the status that came with it.

"And that sweater," she continued. "Have you ever seen anything so horrendous?"

"That's one of ours," piped in Jesse Jonsen—the one in the blue jeans. "We sell those at Bullseye."

All Liz could do was glare at her. Liz saved a more intense dirty look for Berger, one that said, "How dare you sell this crap in our stores? It never would have happened when I was a buyer!"

Liz hated Berger because he put profit ahead of the product. She joined Bullseye twenty years earlier as an assistant buyer because she loved the quirky charm of their products. Buyers traveled the world to find small factories that could produce low-cost household products and clothing that had their own unique style. She would never forget her first trip to Taipei to look for a line of women's spring shoes. The idea was to create low-end "chic" merchandise that women could blend with their designer clothes.

But since Berger took over, that feeling of fun with a strong fashion sense disappeared. When the recession hit, he cut most overseas travel. And instead of investing in fun products or advertising, he expanded the grocery sections and turned Bullseye into a convenience store on steroids. The greedy pig.

Jesse didn't care about fashion, not since she was a teenager anyway. She wore a black off-brand blazer with a red turtleneck. And of course, blue jeans. She was more concerned with comfort than dressing for success. She took her job more seriously than her appearance. Her dark brown hair was cut in a pixie style, which—combined with her youthful face—made her look like a teenager, even though she was in her early thirties. Jesse was also a good foot shorter than Liz, so when the two of them walked down the hallway together, people joked it was "Bring Your Daughter to Work Day."

Liz was still riled up. "That sweater is totally inappropriate," she said. "I haven't seen anything this bad since…" And then she looked over at Berger's ill-fitting toupee. He looked every bit the CEO, trim and fit for a man in his mid-fifties, tailored suits, good tan. But that stupid hairpiece…

"Ryan, what do you think of the presenter?" asked Liz, determined to quit talking before she said something that might offend Berger.

Ryan MacMillan was director of server operations at Bullseye, Inc., reporting directly to the CIO. An important title that meant Ryan was a Windows system administrator. At age thirty-seven, he did his best to blend into the corporate culture with his crisp new Dockers and buttoned-down pinstripe shirts. He enjoyed the tech challenges and prestige from overseeing thousands of servers deployed across the country. Especially the prestige.

"This guy's a total idiot," said Ryan. "He still wears his phone on his belt. Nobody does that anymore. I don't. Besides, I know all this stuff. The only reason this meeting isn't a total washout is the company paid for lunch. And the chicken was pretty good. This time."

"We don't have to worry at Bullseye because we have state-of-the-art security and an outfit in India monitoring all our Internet traffic 24/7. If anything looks suspicious, they'll contact Jesse."

"Whoopee," thought Jesse. Before the recession she headed Bullseye's fraud department. Those were the good old days, when her team was one of the best in the country. But then Berger outsourced the entire department to Bangalore to save a few bucks. His bonus went up again that year. Jesse was reduced to monitoring the monitors. Her job wasn't fun anymore.

"Well I think he's making some good points," said Jesse. "The criminal mind never stops. They enjoy finding new ways to take advantage of clueless people. That's a big part of their motivation—along with the money, of course."

"How come you know so much about the criminal mind?" asked Liz.

Jesse ignored that question.

"You know, I bought that same sweater for my brother last Christmas," said Jesse. "And look, this Barkley guy's going prematurely bald, but he's man enough not to try to hide it."

Berger snapped his head around and gave Jesse a dirty look.

Jesse bit her lip to keep from laughing, and fixed her eyes on the podium.

"Credit-card fraud may be a very small problem for the average retailer, but if you get hit, you get hit big. We've had periodic major data breaches for nearly thirty years, starting with Sears TRW—the credit rating agency—where crooks exposed ninety million credit histories to card forgers."

"Ridiculous," said Berger. "What's anybody going to do with ninety million cards? Even if you started using twenty of them every day, it would still take years and years."

"Just over twelve thousand," said Jesse. "But you're not thinking like a criminal. They don't use all the cards themselves any more than drug lords consume all of their drugs. They find middlemen who imprint batches of the numbers onto phony cards, and then sell them to consumers. I think you'd call it a retail business model."

Berger did a slow burn and frowned in her general direction. He thought to himself, "If she's expecting a holiday bonus this year, she's nuts."

"...Even after all those fixes, crooks hit ninety-four million T.J. Maxx customers in 2007. The Heartland Payment Systems breach in 2008 exposed

130 million cards—and they're a company that processes credit-card payments! Sony was hit for several million card numbers in 2011, and just last week—say, how many of you follow the online blog Lincoln on Security?"

A half dozen hands went up around the room, including Jesse's.

"Anyone interested in Internet security should read Henry Lincoln's blog. He's an investigative reporter who turned his aim on the vast dark side of the Internet. He knows more than anyone about the patterns of criminal behavior in the underground chat rooms and websites.

"Well then, a few of you know already that last week Lincoln reported that Adobe had a breach of 3.8 million cards. It's not over, folks. The pattern in all of these cases is that the crooks don't always try to go in the front door and attack your system head-on. More and more they're finding weak spots though third-party vendors and infiltrating your systems through the back door.

"So in closing, I'd like to leave you with the wise words that the mother told the son who sat down on a freshly painted bench: watch your breeches!"

Jerry couldn't help but smile at his pun, and he was pleasantly surprised to hear a few chuckles mixed in with the groans. All that was soon drowned out by applause, once everybody woke up and figured out Jerry was done speaking.

People started getting up from their tables, but Ryan MacMillan stayed anchored in his seat with his clenched hands squeezing the arms of his chair in anger.

"What? No dessert?!"

Jesse ignored him and went up to the front of the room to greet the speaker. Several men in cheap suits surrounded Jerry and shook his hand while taking one of his business cards. Liz and Berger headed for the escalator. Ryan eventually discovered the self-serve dessert table on the other end of the room and went on a mission for cookies.

Jesse waited for a gap in the crowd and then plunged forward to shake hands with Jerry. He gave her such a big smile that she felt a little tongue-tied. She rehearsed a clever way to congratulate him, but all she could blurt out was, "I like your tennis shoes."

Delighted, Jerry beamed back, "Thanks, I like your jeans."

Awkward silence followed.

Figuring he'd said something stupid, Jerry was determined not to say another word. They continued to shake hands until Jesse murmured "Thanks" and then headed for the door.

After a few minutes, the meeting room was mostly empty, and Jerry stood chatting with a few remaining small business owners. Then out of the corner of his eye, he saw the servers starting to clear away the food table. He abruptly abandoned his cohorts and ran over to the dessert table.

"Hey, wait a minute! I need a couple of those!" He grabbed two oranges. "Thanks for waiting, ma'am."

"Sure, whatever," the pink-haired server replied.

It was an unusually warm day for mid-February in Minneapolis and an outside walk looked inviting. So instead of using the skyway, he rode the escalator down to the main lobby and stepped outside onto South 2nd Avenue. The fresh air felt invigorating. He crossed 2nd Avenue and followed the snow-shoveled walkway into a glass pod above the underground parking garage, and walked downstairs to find his car.

And then he realized he didn't park in the underground ramp. He had parked on the street, across 12th street, one block away. "Dork," he said to himself as he walked back up the stairs.

He remembered he wanted some cereal to eat in the car on the way to a customer appointment early the next morning. "No sense driving somewhere," he thought. "As long as I'm already out walking, may as well just head down the street and buy some at Bullseye."

So instead of crossing 12th Street to his car in the metered parking in front of the ramp, he followed 12th Street to Nicollet Mall and walked the two and a half blocks to the store. He found his cereal and got into the express checkout lane. He must have stared at the short woman in front of him for a solid minute before he realized it was the Bullseye lady from the luncheon who liked his tennis shoes.

Without thinking he blurted out, "Hey lady, I like your jeans!"

She instantly turned around and was ready to slap him. "What's wrong with you, assho—oh, it's you. Hey, tennis shoes!"

They both laughed. No awkward silence now.

"So you big shots at Bullseye actually patronize your own stores, huh?"

"Well, I'm not exactly a big shot, and I'm not sure how long I'll be working for them anyway."

"Moving on up, huh?"

"More like moving on out."

They went quickly through the line and swiped their cards to pay for their purchases.

"Want to grab some coffee?" Jesse asked. "I'm not exactly anxious to get back to my office. Can you spare a few minutes?"

"Sure," Jerry replied. "I have unlimited time on my meter."

"Unlimited time?"

"Sure, it's Presidents' Day, February 18th."

"Presidents' Day? I don't get it."

"Presidents' Day's a municipal holiday. In Minneapolis, all the parking meters are free on holidays. That's one reason I said yes to the Retail Council today, free parking. I don't like paying twelve bucks to park in some ramp."

"Smart. How about this Charbucks? Their cafes are connected with quite a few Bullseyes."

"I'd rather go across the street to Manitou Coffee, if you don't mind. They're a client. And they give me a 10-percent discount."

"Don't tell me you fix espresso machines on the side?"

"I wish. No, they had an issue and I took care of it."

"What happened?"

"The owner's a franchisee with five stores in Minneapolis, and all of a sudden last spring he discovers his busiest store isn't making any money. Or hardly any. At first he thought it was employee theft, but then I discovered the only money they could account for was cash sales. The debit and credit-card sales total was a solid zero. Some days negative. With employee theft, it's the other way around. They take the cash. It turned out to be some two-bit bozos. They'd sit in the shop all day on their laptops. What they were doing was getting into the point-of-sale system using the store's own Wi-Fi, and then refunding their credit cards. When random customers bought a sandwich or a coffee, they refunded double or triple the sale amount to their own cards. They spread it out all day long with different credit cards and small transactions so nobody noticed it. The more the store sold, the more money those clowns made."

"How'd they get in?"

"The Wi-Fi was wide open and the point-of-sale vendor must have delivered the systems with factory-default passwords."

"Unbelievable. So then what happened?"

"We called law enforcement and nothing happened."

"You're kidding!"

"Nope. I'm still mad about that. But I promise you they're locked down now."

Jesse shook her head. By now, they were at the counter. Jesse ordered a latte. Jerry ordered a cup of tap water. They walked to a table and sat down.

"Bullseye must have thousands of POS systems," said Jerry.

"Yeah, about 20,000 of them."

"Wow. And they all run an old version of Windows, right?"

"Yeah."

"So they must be prime targets."

"Exactly."

"What are you guys doing about it?"

"Not enough. I tried to sell Liz on isolating the store POS systems so nobody can put any software on them we don't want. Especially after that *Lincoln on Security* post about a new worm that supposedly can steal credit-card numbers from POS systems."

"Yeah, I saw that. Nasty. I wouldn't want to be in the middle of one of those."

"That's what I told her. But Liz doesn't know what a worm is. She's a retailer at heart and doesn't understand technology. And when she learned my proposal cost money, she said if it didn't directly contribute to retail sales, it would have to wait."

"This must be driving you crazy."

"Yup. Can you keep a secret?"

"Of course. I work in security, don't I?"

"When I get back to my office, I'm submitting my two-weeks' notice. Uncle Sam Bank made me an offer last Friday to work in their fraud department. It's my dream job."

"But what about Bullseye? Why isn't that a dream job?"

"It used to be, until Berger took over and farmed out the guts of our online fraud department to India. Instead of running the operation, I'm an overpriced secretary. To make things worse, our C-level executives think Bullseye is invincible. They've never been hit hard and think they never will. They're more than arrogant. They don't have a clue how the criminal mind works."

"And you do?"

"Can you keep another secret?"

"Sure, I'll bury it inside the first one."

"I learned about the criminal mind from firsthand experience."

"What? You're friends with a criminal? Don't tell me you married one?"

"It's worse than that. I was one."

"You? No way."

"I was young, very young. As a little girl I was able to sense how to take advantage of people who were clueless. I called them suckers. It was from an old comedy movie I saw on TV late one night when I was supposed to be asleep. This guy had a big nose and was very funny. He would say, 'Never give a sucker an even break.'"

"That was W.C. Fields."

"That's right. So that became my mantra, 'Never give a sucker an even break.' I got a thrill figuring out how to cheat people. I'd steal candy, toys, little things. As I got older it would be clothes and CDs. It wasn't because we were poor or anything. I did it for the pure excitement of it. It was a game."

"What happened?"

"Well, I wasn't careful enough, or maybe I just quit caring about it. You know, I was a teenager by then. I told my mom I could afford nice clothes and things because I worked at Dairy Queen, and one day she went out to buy a cone and the manager told her he'd never heard of me."

"So your mom sent you up the river?"

"Not exactly. Because I cooperated I stayed out of hard-core reform school. They sent me to a sort of halfway house for juvenile offenders."

"That must have been terrible."

"It wasn't so bad. The people were nice, and that's where I learned about computers. Part of our service learning program was to repair and upgrade old computers so they could be used in inner-city schools."

"Nice."

"And that's where I learned to make lemonade."

"Huh?"

"You know, lemonade, as in the old saying, 'When life gives you lemons, make lemonade.' That means you take a bad thing and turn it into a good thing. In my case, the bad thing was I was born with a criminal mind. I just decided to use it for a good purpose. Thinking like a criminal makes me a very good fraud detector. My new thrill is outthinking the criminals. They're the suckers now. I try to be one step ahead of them, and I'm not about to give them an even break."

"Very commendable. I wish you all the best in your new job. I'll bet Bullseye will miss you."

"They won't even know I'm gone, believe me."

"This is all very interesting. Tell you what. Why don't you take my business card, in case you ever need my services over there."

"Sure, you never know."

"Wait a minute. I don't even know your name. I can't just call over there and ask for Ms. Blue Jeans."

"Maybe you could. I'm not planning to change my wardrobe. Just kidding. I'm Jesse Jonsen. Here, I'll give you my old Bullseye card. You can cross out the office number, but the cell phone will still be good."

"Pleased to meet you, Jesse."

And for the second time that day, Jerry and Jesse shook hands.

***

Two weeks later, on the seventeenth floor of Bullseye corporate headquarters, Ryan MacMillan poked his head into Liz Isaacs' office.

"Well, she's gone," Ryan announced in a singsong voice.

"Who's gone?" asked Liz.

"Jesse Jonsen, you know, the petite fashion maven."

"Oh, her," laughed Liz.

"So when can I post the job opening to replace her?" asked Ryan. "You've been putting me off for two weeks."

"Oh, that. Um, at our executive meeting this morning Berger announced a hiring freeze—with the exception of salespeople. It'll have to wait until January. Can you manage?"

"When have I ever failed you? I'll just use an intern. I hired a good one for spring quarter, Danielle Weyerhauser."

"That's what I like to hear. On the brighter side, Berger mentioned you in the meeting, too."

"He did?"

"Yeah. Well, actually the marketing department gave an update on how well your new database is working to track the buying habits of our Bullseye Card users. Berger said it's all thanks to our IT department, and you in particular. Now we can run personalized promotions for each customer, both online and hard copy. He thinks it's coming together just in time to boost holiday sales."

"Great! I hope this means a bonus."

Liz didn't want to tell him that she was the only one getting a bonus in their department this year. Time to change the subject.

"Did you delete Jesse Jonsen's email account?"

"Don't worry," replied Ryan. "She's been a nonperson for two hours already."

Rousseau Plumbing and Mechanical

Spring would soon be in the air in upstate New York near the shores of Lake Champlain.

"Thank God for Bullseye!" thought Max Rousseau. "And for my nephew Maurice. Maybe now I can retire someday without living in a trailer."

Max, who was a few days from his sixty-seventh birthday, looked every bit his age with his weathered face and gray hair. The founder and CEO of Rousseau Plumbing and Mechanical of Plattsburgh, New York, sat in his tiny crowded office wearing his plumber's overalls as usual. He squinted through his dirty bifocals as he read and reread his latest online bank statement showing payments from Bullseye Corp. for plumbing and mechanical services. The world would be better if everything were still on paper, but if he needed a computer to read numbers like these, he could tolerate one.

A year ago, his only retirement plan was picking good numbers for the Powerball lottery twice a week. That all changed when his younger brother Franck left a phone message.

"Hello, Max, warm greetings from your little brother in Guadeloupe. And I mean warm. We're having a record heat wave—but I'm sure you don't want to hear about that because I see it's still freezing up there." He laughed. "Listen, since you're still working, give my son Maurice a call. He's become a big-shot contractor in Montreal and they're looking for a French-speaking troubleshooter who knows plumbing. Give him a call, okay? And when are you and Edith ever going to make it down to the Caribbean? Melanie and I have been waiting five years! Bye-bye, big brother!"

Max always knew when his brother called, because he always called on Sundays at 9:00 p.m. And Max was always too embarrassed to answer. Max and Franck grew up working for their father's plumbing company in Montreal, but Franck went off to study architecture while Max inherited the company. Max had big plans for expanding the business, but then he met Edith, a tall, pigtailed blonde from the US who had come to Canada to study French. The first time he gazed into her stunning blue eyes, he was hooked. But after a year of marriage she realized she hated the big city and was homesick for her parents, who had a dairy farm just outside of Plattsburgh. So the Rousseau Plumbing and Mechanical World Headquarters relocated across the border. It was just one hour south of Montreal, but a world away. The change made Edith happy. His company, however, suffered. Too much competition in the area. He'd had maybe five employees at his peak, but after the recession it was down to just Max and Edith.

"What have I got to lose?" he thought. "I'll give Maurice a call."

He pulled his trusty rotary dial phone to the center of his desk and put his finger to work. Maurice was glad to hear from him, but sounded anxious.

"These crazy Americans," said Maurice. "They suddenly want to invade Canada with a hundred big-box discount stores, and they hire me as their general contractor."

"That sounds good," said Max. "What's the problem?"

"The problem is they don't know what they're doing. It's too much, too fast. We break our backs getting the first twenty stores ready to open, and suddenly their CEO decides he wants to double the grocery sections. That means I have to retrofit new refrigeration units on the existing stores and reconfigure the ones under construction. I need someone with your skills right away. You're not too busy, are you?"

"Well, I've really got my sleeves rolled up, and today I didn't have time to sit down," said Max.

He was not about to tell Maurice he had spent all day at an apartment complex unclogging six toilets.

"But for my favorite nephew, I can clear my calendar."

"Great! I'll email you the log-in credentials for Bullseye Corp. Oh, they have a mobile app for it, too, if you prefer. If you have any trouble, just text me. You're familiar with Bullseye, aren't you?"

"Sure. They've got a new store here in Plattsburgh. It's big."

"Great, Uncle Max. I'll be in touch."

Max was overcome with conflicting emotions after that call. He was excited about the prospect of making some real money. But the idea of dealing with any sort of technology made him feel dizzy and nauseous. "Email?" "Mobile app?" "Text me?" "Log-in?"

"Too many people hide behind too much technology today," he thought. He took pride in telling customers and friends at the local Chamber of Commerce that he was old school. Old school meant doing things right. A man's word should be his bond. A good look in the eye was better than a credit check, and all his business deals were settled with a handshake. That was the way Dad had taught him. Do the work, collect a check, put it in the bank, pay your bills, and keep what's left over for a rainy day.

Why did he need a bunch of high-tech gadgets for that?

"If I have to deal with high tech with Bullseye, I'll have Edith handle it. She does all the bookkeeping and correspondence and billing anyway. If she has any problems she can always call *him*. I'm not about to."

Edith's eyes were still blue, and she continued to wear pigtails, only now her hair was gray and her brow was wrinkled. *Him* was their son Jerome, who now worked as a computer programmer in Dallas. Max barely talked to *him* anymore. He was still angry about being suckered into buying a computer system for his business in the late '90s. Everyone in his Chamber of Commerce about that time was gaga over this new sensation called the "Internet." They all wanted websites so they could be on the Internet and sell goods and services to people in Europe or Asia or Australia or God-knows-where. "The Yellow Pages are obsolete," they'd said. "If your business doesn't have a website, it may as well not exist."

Max was skeptical, but then Jerome came home from college that summer and all he could talk about was the Internet. He easily sold his mother on the scheme, and then the two teamed up on Max. He had been outnumbered. So Max took out a mortgage on his hunting lodge in northern Quebec, and spent $50,000 for Jerome to build a website and install a server and computer system in his office. At the end of the summer Jerome went back to school and Max was left with a website that nobody looked at and mortgage payments he couldn't afford.

Edith loved it. She learned to use word processing programs instead of the typewriter, and the spreadsheet programs helped her with her bookkeeping. She even learned how to do email, and eventually got so she could add attachments. And she put—what did she call it—a shortcut on the computer in Max's office so he could look at banking transactions. But *he* probably did it for her. Whenever she got stuck or had a problem, she'd call Jerome. *Him.* He who didn't want to take over the plumbing business. He who never learned French. He who was starting to develop a Texan drawl. *Him.*

***

Much had changed in the year since that conversation with Maurice. Instead of cleaning out toilets, Max now supervised several crews across eastern Canada redoing plumbing and HVAC connections for the grocery units at Bullseyes.

He realized almost immediately he needed cell phones for himself and each of his workers. Edith called Jerome for advice on which phones to buy and what wireless plans to use. And now Max had to figure out how to use this new little computer he held in his hand.

"If these phones are so smart, why can't I make a simple phone call on one?"

Jerome came home for Christmas and tried to talk Max into updating the computers and server. Max wasn't buying. He was still bitter over losing his hunting lodge. His brother Franck had stepped in and bought it before the bank foreclosed on it, just to keep it in the family.

"But Dad, they're antiques," Jerome insisted. "You can't even install the latest antivirus software."

"I wasted good money on that system, and I'm not spending another cent."

And that was why Edith spent each workday in front of a ten-year-old, barely functional computer.

***

Max stared at the monthly electronic payment summary on that accursed computer screen in his office. Real checks would have been better, but electronic money was better than no money. Edith broke his reverie when she brought the latest cell phone bill from Champlain Wireless into his office. "You wanted to see this, Max?"

"Yeah. Why do those phones cost so much?" Max asked while looking at the document. "What are these things? Roaming charges, international data plan—I don't get it. Can you figure it out for me?"

"Why don't I just call Jerome? He'll know."

"No!"

Max looked again at the cell phone bill, and then relented.

"Okay, call *your* son. Just figure it out so we can maybe save some money."

"Don't worry, Max. I'll handle it."

"Thank you, my dear."

Edith went to her desk, turned on her computer, and waited. She waited some more. Now just a little bit more. And a little more after that. "What does 'XP' really stand for, anyway?" she asked herself for about the millionth time. She would have to remember to ask Jerome. Finally: "Press Control+Alt+Delete to log on." And now another agonizing wait until she could do something useful. It was the morning ritual, and the most frustrating part of her job.

When her computer finally awoke, she checked her email and found a message in her inbox from Champlain Wireless, with the subject line, "Account Expired." The message was short and direct:

```
CHAMPLAIN WIRELESS UPDATE

You must update your log-in info to maintain
service. View attachment and continue. Thank
you!
MESSAGE-ID-1HDSA-DHAS871G-DAHS671-AJ12D
```

The message looked important, so she clicked on the attachment, "UpdateLoginInfo.html," and found that familiar and frustrating hourglass symbol on her screen. It lasted a few seconds and... nothing. The hourglass symbol just disappeared. She tried again and the hourglass came on and disappeared again. Faster this time.

She wasn't sure whether she did it right, so she called Champlain Wireless to make sure their account was active. They assured her it was, but the person she talked to didn't know anything about an email update.

"That figures," Edith thought. "They never tell the receptionist anything. Now what time is it in Texas? I need to call Jerome."

***

Champlain Wireless could not have known about Edith's email because it didn't come from Champlain Wireless. Edith's email originated in Florida and routed through China on the way to her inbox. It was part of a "phishing" expedition, orchestrated by a gangster in St. Petersburg, Russia, named Ivan Tarski and a loosely connected group of criminal specialists, looking for somebody like Edith to help find a fortune.

When Edith clicked on her email attachment, a few data packets traveled at the speed of light from Edith's computer to Tehran, Iran, joining her computer with thousands of other drones in a rented robot army. Almost immediately, another tiny dot appeared on a dynamic heat map of the world on Ivan Tarski's computer screen in St. Petersburg, representing the newest member of Tarski's rented botnet. Tarski stared at his heat-map screen the same way Max stared at his Bullseye payments screen. It was the same way the city's namesake, Peter the Great, would gaze upon his royal troops when they gathered for battle. But unlike troops commanded by Peter the Great, most of Tarski's rented troops would never know they were part of Tarski's army.

Tarski's aim was to invade a large retail company, find a weak link in that company's defenses, and seize the data of many millions of credit-card numbers. Ivan Tarski would make history as a modern day czar. His greatest ally in this conquest would be an innocent, blue-eyed woman with gray pigtails near the shore of Lake Champlain, half a world away. But for now, Edith's computer silently waited for orders from a command and control server in Tehran, Iran, rented to a gangster in St. Petersburg, Russia.

Tarski's new recruit received its first orders the next morning when Edith turned on her computer. It took even longer than usual to start up that morning because it secretly downloaded and installed a *keylogging* program from an obscure download site in Iran to record every keystroke Edith made on her computer. From that point forward, any time Edith logged into a website or other system, that keylogging program scooped up her log-in information and uploaded it to an FTP server in St. Petersburg, Russia.

Max should have listened to Jerome. A spam-filtering service may have blocked that email from ever arriving. And if it had gotten through, a good antivirus program may have stopped the attachment from opening, or at least warned Edith about it. If Edith had been more astute, she could have checked the email's properties in the header. But Edith didn't know what email headers were, and if she saw one, it would look like hieroglyphics. Even after Edith's computer was compromised, a good firewall at the Rousseau Internet boundary could have flagged suspicious traffic to Iran and Russia.

But Max did not listen to Jerome. There were no layers of defense at Rousseau Plumbing and Mechanical. And that was why an obsolete, barely functional computer, sitting on a cluttered desk in a tiny family business with no secrets inside its computer network anyone cared about, became a key link in a global chain of events that shook the world.

Max should have listened to his son.

Ivan Tarski

Ivan Tarski had always used his official governmental positions to find ways to make real money. Long ago Tarski developed a taste for caviar, vodka, women, and an ever-more-lavish lifestyle unsupportable by a government salary. Under the Soviet Union, he supervised factories and sold "surplus" merchandise on the black market. When the Soviet Union dissolved, he became chief inspector of imports in St. Petersburg. Once again, he collected a certain percentage of "surplus" merchandise, which he resold, and he was also paid handsomely to look the other way for illicit shipments of drugs, weapons, and women. It was profitable for many years, until a political appointee edged him out of his office when Putin came to power. Tarski found himself in charge of St. Petersburg's utilities—power, water, telephones—and the fast-growing infrastructure that served the Internet.

By this time Tarski was in his late forties, but aging gracefully. With his graying hair, ruddy complexion, and growing access to power, he became popular at all the right social events, usually with an attractive woman on his arm.

Always looking for new forms of exploitation, and as a consequence of his new job, he turned his attention to the Internet. He quickly realized the power the Internet would bring to those with the ability and will to exploit it. Immune to national borders, those who harnessed this power would be rich beyond their wildest fantasies.

At first he made money selling privileged government information to organized crime bosses. He gradually gained influence until he became an organized crime boss himself, still constantly looking for bigger targets in the bustling underworld of cybercrime. He found his way into several underground discussion forums and chat rooms and developed a reputation as a cagey and covert investor, betting on projects he thought had a reasonable chance of generating profit.

One early lucrative project was a scheme to extort money from Caribbean gambling websites. It was a work of beauty. Since online gambling in the US was illegal, but many US citizens apparently wished to gamble, websites sprang up in Caribbean countries to service the demand outside the reach of US law. With a few keystrokes and mouse clicks, anyone in the US could visit these sites and bet on sports, the stock market, the weather, or anything else. The sites quickly grew, generating millions of dollars in profits for their expat American owners.

Tarski wanted a piece of this action. He found the key to getting it one day when he met a character who used the handle "Alma" in an underground chat room. Alma, a.k.a. Bahir Mustafa of Iran, claimed to control a network of several thousand computers around the world. These computers would run any program Alma asked them to run.

"What if," Tarski asked, "these computers from all around the world were to each run a program that would cumulatively flood those Caribbean websites with traffic?" Then their American customers would not be able to access them and the website operators would be cut off from their source of revenue. They would pay dearly for protection from such interference. And Tarski would provide that protection, in return for a share of the revenue.

True to his promises, Mustafa sent the appropriate instructions to his network of compromised computers, and within seconds, key US offshore gambling websites went offline.

US law enforcement refused to help these website operators; Caribbean law enforcement was unable to intervene; and Russian law enforcement did not care. With nowhere else to turn, the sites reluctantly accepted Tarski's generous offer. It was a perfect money-making opportunity, and it worked for several months until the website operators developed countermeasures.

Tarski smiled inwardly as he remembered that exhilarating adventure. First the mistrust, then uncertainty, and finally euphoria as it all came together. Anyone could easily control a network of computers around the world! Of course, he paid Mustafa a small fee and a bonus. His only question was, "What's next?"

While shopping for ideas in another underground website, he saw an ad for GreenPOS, a program to extract credit-card numbers from POS (point-of-sale) systems. This was intriguing. Imagine controlling a large share of the retail POS terminals around the world. How would he accomplish such a task? Assuming this credit-card-extraction program worked, how would he introduce it into POS systems under the noses of the retailers who operated them?

Exploiting this opportunity would require careful planning and reconnaissance. And he would need some help. GreenPOS could yield many American dollars by providing thousands, maybe millions of credit-card numbers. But he needed to find a way to introduce this new software into the POS systems of major retailers.

POS systems—modern-day cash registers—were really just computers with special software and hardware added. Most ran an old version of a Windows operating system lacking the latest security patches. Penetrating these systems would not be a problem. Finding them would be more challenging. Any competent retailer would locate those systems behind a company firewall and regulate contact with them.

Many people misunderstood Internet firewall systems, which were really just routers blocking unsolicited traffic from entering a network. A store might have a series of internal computers, maybe some servers, and a connection to the Internet. The store would place a special router at the boundary between its internal network and the Internet, and install rules in this router, regulating what comes in.

A conversation over the Internet was similar to a conversation in real life. One person asks a question, another person answers. A firewall typically only blocks unsolicited questions. This is why users behind a firewall can still access websites across the Internet. A user inside the store accesses a website and the website returns an answer. The firewall must allow the answer. But if a website tried to send an unsolicited question to the store, any properly configured firewall would block it.

Tarski quickly realized that trying to attack any POS system directly from the outside would be fruitless. Instead of a frontal assault sure to fail, he would find and exploit any architectural weakness and attack from a different direction.

One possibility was a company's website. Websites must be available to the public, and so a firewall must have rules allowing unsolicited contact with them. Perhaps there was a website lacking the latest security patches where he could pose a question formatted in such a way that the website would grant him access to its server. There were thousands of possibilities for such questions. Databases of known exploits were readily available, along with automated programs to try a database of exploits against another database of known websites. From there, he could explore the network behind it and search for POS terminals or other vulnerable systems.

Email also provided possibilities. When users retrieved email, they invited whatever was imbedded in that email onto their computers. If Tarski could somehow imbed a useful program in that email and entice users to run it, perhaps he could gain a foothold inside one of these networks to start searching for POS systems.

With the wisdom of a military strategist, Tarski decided to launch simultaneous attacks. He would go after corporate websites and email users at the same time. He made the rounds of illicit chat rooms and recruited a team of veteran cybercriminals, each with their own specialty. Tarski knew them by their skill, not by their true identities.

There was "Duceml," a.k.a. Frank Urbino, an American in Miami who called himself "King of Spam." Duceml was an acronym for his specialty: delivers unsolicited commercial email. He harvested millions of email addresses and kept them in a database, indexed by demographics, region, and dozens of other attributes so he could design tailor-made fake emails appealing to individual interests or impersonating businesses common to the victim's postal code.

Duceml often relayed his email through "Wongladee," a.k.a. Wai Jiande, who operated a cybercafé in Shanghai as a cover for an underground bulk-email relay service with the tacit approval of her biggest customer, the Chinese government.

Tarski already knew "Alma." Alma would again rent access to his botnet comprised of thousands of compromised computers under his control. For this project, he would also provide a disguised keylogger program for Duceml to attach to tailored email messages routed through Wongladee's relay service.

And finally, "Livefree," a.k.a. Turlach Flanagan, an alcoholic from Belfast who lost his family to a bomb meant for him. He specialized in hacking into the databases behind websites and extracting their data.

Using this global network of specialists, Tarski would fund the operation, run it, and take almost all the reward.

He still needed to fill one more missing hole. When data started pouring in from the email and website attacks, Tarski would need something to accept it all, somewhere to store it, and a telecom path with plenty of capacity to handle it.

For many years he groomed a special "nephew" for just this purpose. Yuri Makerov was just a young boy when his parents were in a terrible car crash. His father was killed, and his mother barely survived and never walked again. For some reason, Tarski became their secret benefactor. Even though his mother, Sofia, would spend the rest of her life in a wheelchair, Yuri grew up without suffering from dire poverty. Tarski finally introduced himself to the boy as he was about to enter college. He encouraged Yuri to study computer science, and even sent him to study in the West. It was time to collect on that investment.

Yuri was now a young man in his late twenties, slender, and awkward in social settings. But he had a big heart, and that impressed a pretty black-haired temp worker at his office, Oksana Sobchak. She had just turned eighteen and moved from a small town to St. Petersburg. The big city intimidated her, and Yuri was the first person who showed her any kindness. She became Yuri's first girlfriend, and when her temp job was over and she needed a place to stay, Yuri invited her to come live with him and his mother. At first Oksana praised Yuri for being so kind to his mother, but eventually she thought he spent too much time looking after her. She was partly jealous, and partly disgusted. But she had nowhere else to go, so she made the best of it. Besides, Yuri was so kind.

One afternoon Yuri was surprised to receive a call from Tarski.

"My dear nephew, I trust you're doing well!"

"Uncle Ivan! It's a pleasure to hear from you! To what do I owe this great honor?"

"Well, it has been so long since I saw you last. I thought it was time to renew our acquaintance."

"I'd be delighted."

"I was thinking of a little evening on the town, perhaps the Troika, or some other cabaret of your choice."

"That would be excellent. I've never been there because it's so—shall we say—luxurious."

"Think nothing of it. Please be my guest. And are you married? Do you have a girlfriend? Bring her along."

"Yes, I'm engaged to a beautiful girl. I would very much like you to meet Oksana."

"Wonderful! There will be another couple there, my assistant Fyodor Renkin and his wife."

"We look forward to it!"

Oksana was pleased to enjoy a gourmet dinner at a premium nightclub in central St. Petersburg. Tarski paid for the finest vodka, caviar, and roast lamb. Oksana was self-conscious about whether her red silk dress was fancy enough for the occasion and embarrassed by Yuri's old gray suit. The sleeves and the pant-legs were both several centimeters too short. But Fyodor was dressed almost as elegantly as Tarski. He was handsome, too. Although Oksana found him charming, there was something about Fyodor that Yuri didn't like. And Yuri didn't trust Fyodor any more than he trusted Tarski. Tarski was accompanied by a beautiful blonde about half his age, Natalya. She wore a low-cut evening gown of shimmering gold, and constantly leaned on Tarski's shoulder and carried a drink in her right hand.

"I'm sorry my wife could not make it tonight," apologized Fyodor as they sat down at the table Tarski reserved. "Our youngest son became ill and she decided to stay home with him."

"I trust he'll be fine," said Tarski. "I would like to discuss some business with my nephew here. Fyodor, would you be a gentleman and ask Oksana to dance?"

Without hesitation, Fyodor rose from the table and bowed before Oksana. She averted her eyes and blushed, but then sprang to her feet as the two of them laughed their way to the dance floor. Yuri gave both a dirty look, but they didn't notice. Tarski pretended he didn't notice either.

And then he turned to Natalya. "I see your lipstick is smeared. You may wish to touch it up."

"Anything for you, my darling." She grabbed her cigarettes and her drink and headed toward the ladies' room.

"Yuri, my boy, how you have blossomed into manhood! I'm proud of you and your accomplishments."

"Thank you, uncle. I could not have accomplished any of it without your help."

"It was nothing. I think of your mother often. How's she doing?"

"As well as can be expected. As you requested, I never told her of the bank account you set up for her, but of course, she suspects you're behind the money that keeps her alive."

"And I'll continue to support your mother. But I have another matter I wish to discuss with you."

"Yes?"

"I'm conducting business research and gathering data from various sources. For this purpose, I need a server with a large Internet connection. This special research is confidential and needs to remain secret. I will, of course, pay for everything you need to set it up, but its real purpose must remain a secret. You'll help me with this research?"

"Uncle, this is highly unusual."

"I know I ask much of you, but I offer much in return. Consider it a request from the City of St. Petersburg. We need you to set up a server to hold the data as it arrives from collection points around the world. I'll use programs on my computer to analyze this data."

"What's the nature of this data?"

"It's classified, but involves information we wish to examine from the West. Surely, now you can see the need for confidentiality with this project."

"Yes. I'll make the necessary arrangements."

"Excellent!"

Before long, data started flowing in from around the world. Tarski's FTP site kept two growing lists: one with log-in credentials users sent to websites, the other with log-in credentials websites expected to see. Each list was worthless by itself. But combined, they were a treasure trove of illicit data.

***

One day during the spring of 2013—nobody knows the exact date—Edith Rousseau logged into the Bullseye Corp. payment system to submit an invoice, just like she had done many times over the past year. As her well-worn instruction sheet said, it was a two-step process. First, she clicked an icon on her screen with "SSL VPN" in the title. She never knew what SSL VPN meant, only that she needed it to submit her invoices. After a few seconds, a log-in window came up in the middle of her screen and she logged in with her username and password. Next, she clicked on another icon that brought up the payments website, where she entered the work order number, description of the work, billing amount, and clicked "Submit." It was all routine.

But this time, the keylogging program hidden in her computer added a new and sinister invisible step to Edith's process. Occupying a barely noticeable corner of the cyberspace inside Edith's computer, the program took notice when Edith launched her SSL VPN program and copied her log-in credentials as she entered them. Immediately after Edith finished logging into that connection, a data packet containing her log-in credentials began a journey across the Internet to an FTP server mounted in an equipment rack in a data center in St. Petersburg, Russia. It was all over in less than three seconds.

However, when Edith clicked the icon on her screen to log into the Bullseye payment website, the keylogging program in her computer had no way to record which Internet site she accessed. It could only monitor which keys she pressed on her keyboard. It stole her log-in credentials, but not the site to which those credentials belonged. It was like stealing a set of car keys, but not knowing which car they belonged to.

Tarski's website attacks also stole log-in credentials, but they were from Internet sites, not from users—and the passwords were generally either encrypted or hashed, rendering them unusable by themselves. It was like stealing a warehouse full of cars, but no keys.

The challenge was to match keys with cars.

***

Yuri's phone rang as he left work.

"Hello, Yuri, this is Uncle Ivan. I require your assistance once more."

"Yes, Uncle. How may I help?"

"I need you to be a matchmaker."

"What? Are you becoming a wedding planner?"

"In a way. We are looking for log-in credentials to Western retailers. We have one list of credentials people enter. We have another list of credentials websites expect to receive, but with garbled passwords. One list has usernames and passwords; the other list has websites and usernames, but garbled passwords. We need to match the usernames and produce one list with websites, usernames, and passwords."

"Uncle, this is a basic database join operation. I can make this program for you."

"Thank you, my favorite nephew."

Every few days, Tarski ran Yuri's program to match user credentials with website credentials. It was an intensive operation to compare millions of user credentials with web credentials from thousands of candidate sites. It would not have been feasible to do it manually. But with modern computers and Yuri's programming skills, the job was simple—if not tedious.

And one day, Tarski found a match. It seemed user ERousseau with password 04272005EjR from a computer with an IP address in the northeastern United States matched an Internet site named https://payments.bullseyestores.com. *"Magnificent!"* he cried as he opened a bottle of rare champagne. "I toast you, ERousseau, the key to my future wealth!"

And with that Tarski lifted his glass and drank.

***

Ivan Tarski was not the only person monitoring those FTP server logs. Yuri Makerov was nobody's fool. That server was in his data center and he answered to people who would want to know its real purpose. And after Uncle Ivan asked Yuri to write this program to match log-in credentials with websites, Yuri knew its real purpose. "Extracting information from the West, eh, Uncle?" he thought. "You're extracting server log-in credentials for every large retailer in Europe and North America on one list, and user credentials from all over the world in another list. And I'm helping you match them. So this is how a mid-level official with the City of St. Petersburg pays for women and houses across Russia."

The scope of this operation was breathtaking. And Yuri wanted a piece of it. And more.

Dark Secrets

Twenty years earlier, shortly after the Soviet Union broke up, Yuri was a young boy in grade school. He barely remembered his father, some sort of business broker to the old Soviet factories and stores that were sold to private investors. Uncle Ivan was a family friend who offered bribes to win favors for "preferred" investors, in return for a healthy kickback. Yuri's life changed forever one day when the school headmaster asked him to step outside the classroom. There had been a horrible car accident. Father was dead and mother was in critical condition. Shards of glass flew through her face, and the impact severed her lower spine. She would never walk again—if she survived. Yuri stayed with relatives for nearly a year while his mother healed. When she returned home, he devoted his life to looking after her. His childhood ended when he became a caretaker at the age of nine.

When Yuri was eighteen years old, his mother judged it was time for him to learn the truth.

"Yuri, I'm sorry for being a bad mother."

"You're hardly a bad mother. You cared for me to the best of your ability."

"You don't know everything. And now I must tell you. And then I'll ask something of you in return. Or, more accurately, beg something of you in return."

"Mother, what are you talking about?"

"Things are not always as they seem."

"How so?"

"Yuri, I'm a sinner and not worthy to live in this world."

"You sound like the Christian missionaries flooding our city."

"Because it's true. I committed unspeakable sins. And now I pay the price."

"What sin?"

"Ivan Tarski was my lover."

"What?"

"He was my lover while I was married to your father. Your father and Ivan were rivals in the organization to which they both belonged. When I broke off the relationship with Ivan, he killed your father."

"How can this be? You showed me a copy of the official report. It was a poorly built Lada and Father lost control when the brakes failed."

"And why do you think the brakes failed? Ivan believed that if your father were dead, I would marry him. Ivan telephoned the night before and said he wanted to meet with your father. Alone. I knew what Ivan wanted. I had already made the decision to break it off with Ivan and felt I needed to tell the truth to both of them. So I insisted on riding with your father to that meeting. I was not supposed to be in the car. And Ivan had no intention of meeting with your father. Your father was supposed to die in a tragic and horrible car accident. The brakes failed because Ivan wished it, and men under his control made the brakes fail."

"How can this be?"

"I'm but a poor, crippled, deformed old woman. But I want you to remember me as I was; proud, competent, attractive, and a good mother to my son. I want you to grow strong. Learn all you can. Become powerful. And when the time is right, I want you to push Ivan Tarski down to the depths of hell. Promise me you'll satisfy my request."

"I swear, Mother. Your revenge will be mine."

As Yuri kissed his mother on the cheek, Sofia braced her heart to withhold one final secret, one that Yuri must never hear. She was even afraid to think it, for fear Yuri might sense it. "Ivan Tarski is your true father. But if you knew, you might not seek his downfall."

Hacking the Hacker

Tarski pondered how best to exploit these new log-in credentials. "Try the easy steps first," he thought to himself, so he opened a web browser from his computer and went to https://payments.bullseyestores.com.

After entering ERousseau and her password at the log-in prompt, a helpful pop-up said he was accessing the system for the first time from this computer and asked if he wanted to download the VPN client. Tarski clicked "Yes," and after the download finished a few seconds later, a new, small graphical icon that looked like two green traffic lights connected by a lightning bolt appeared in the system tray area in the lower right corner of his screen.

"What's a VPN?" he wondered to himself as he picked up his cell phone.

"My dear Yuri, I need you right away. Please come to my home at once."

"Uncle Ivan, you could never ask too much. I'll be there right away."

Yuri arrived at Tarski's house within the hour. As Yuri walked in the front door, Tarski handed him a glass filled with vodka and said, "Yuri, what's a VPN?"

"A VPN is a Virtual Private Network. VPNs use private, encrypted tunnels to connect multiple sites. Anyone else tapping into the conversations will see what appears to be gibberish."

Hacking the Hacker

"Ah, now this makes sense. Come to my computer room."

They walked upstairs to a windowless room that seemed to contain more sophisticated equipment than Yuri's office.

"Look at this," said Tarski, pointing to a huge computer screen. "An icon on my computer says I'm connected to the payment system with Bullseye Stores, a large American retailer. This VPN connects my computer to this retailer, yes?"

"Yes. Congratulations, Uncle. You have penetrated a large American company. What do you intend to do?"

Tarski tried to hide his smile. "I'm conducting research."

He was in. Now to find out what "in" really meant.

"May I?" asked Yuri. Tarski stood up and Yuri sat in Tarski's chair in front of the computer. Yuri launched a CMD window and typed the command, **ipconfig/all.**

"What is this program?" Tarski asked.

"We use the Windows CMD program for various command level diagnostics. This command will tell us much about the network to which we are connected." Yuri pointed on the screen to the relevant portion of the command output.

```
C:\Users\Ivan>ipconfig/all
Windows IP Configuration


Host Name. . . . . . . . . . . : Ivant-pc
Primary Dns Suffix. . . . . . : Tarski.local
Node Type. . . . . . . . . . . : Hybrid
IP Routing Enabled. . . . . . : No
WINS Proxy Enabled. . . . . . : No
DNS Suffix Search List. . . . : Tarski.local
                                bullseye.local
Tunnel adapter beyepmt-ssl:
```

```
Connection-specific DNS Suffix : bullseye.local
Description. . . . . . . . . . : beyepmt VPN
Physical Address. . . . . . . : 08-2E-5F-02-2F-6E
DHCP Enabled. . . . . . . . . : Yes
Autoconfiguration Enabled. . . : Yes
IPv4 Address. . . . . . . . . : 10.150.241.176(Preferred)
Subnet Mask. . . . . . . . . : 255.255.248.0
Lease Obtained. . . . . : Wed, Apr. 3, 2013 4:25:31 AM
Lease Expires. . . . . : Thur, Apr. 4, 2013 4:25:31 AM
Default Gateway. . . . . . . : 10.150.240.1
DHCP Server. . . . . . . . . : 10.150.240.2
DNS Servers. . . . . . . . . : 10.1.1.135
                               10.2.1.135
NetBIOS over Tcpip. . . . . . : Enabled
```

Yuri summarized what this all this meant.

"First, the DNS suffix, bullseye.local, suggests you're indeed connected to a segment of Bullseye's internal network.

"The subnet mask—a specific portion of the overall network—suggests this private network supports 8,192 sites, with each site supporting up to 2,046 computers. It's further evidence you're connected to a small subnet within a large network. This is why you need my help. Let's be honest. Why are you penetrating this American retail company?"

"Our government wishes to explore security systems used around the world, and thereby find ways to improve the security of Russian systems. I'm not at liberty to discuss it any further."

"I see," said Yuri, though he didn't believe a word. "Let's continue. The default gateway is a router connecting this network segment—this subnet—with the rest of this large private network and the public Internet. It's an electronic door through which all traffic must pass to get outside this subnet. You need to know more about this gateway."

"Why?"

"Because this organization has a large private network and if you're not careful with your probes, you'll alert them and they'll shut you down."

Stunned, Tarski picked up his vodka glass, took a large sip, and began pacing. As a businessman, of course, Tarski knew about Bullseye—one of the largest retail companies in the world with more than 2,000 stores across North America. Was it really his good fortune to be inside this network, courtesy of ERousseau? If so, there would be thousands of POS terminals and millions of credit cards to make him rich beyond measure. The possibilities were staggering—even beyond his wildest imagination. And even though Yuri was a favorite nephew, Tarski was not ready to share this good fortune. But he needed help.

"How do I find out more?"

"What do you want to find?"

"As I said, I'm not at liberty to discuss it any further."

"Very well. Then I'm unable to help you further."

"Nephew, I require your assistance. I have never asked anything of you until now. But all of Russia will be grateful if you share your expertise for this project."

"Uncle, without knowledge of what you're trying to find, how can I possibly help you look for it?"

"Perhaps we can identify the systems in this network and their functions. Any additional information would be helpful."

Yuri knew what Uncle Ivan wanted to find. Only one answer made sense. He was looking for the store point-of-sale systems with the intent of robbing them. But how? Since Ivan would not share this information on his own, Yuri would find it himself. He came prepared.

"I have some advanced scanning software on this memory card," Yuri said, as he took the memory card from his pocket and inserted it into a USB slot. "Perhaps you'll find it helpful. May I install it on your computer?"

What Tarski did not know was that a few seconds after Yuri inserted his memory card into the USB slot, Tarski's computer dutifully ran the autorun program on the USB card. Autorun programs usually play music or display pictures or video. But this autorun program silently copied and installed its own Trojan horse program from Yuri's memory card onto Tarski's computer. Yuri built this program himself and tested it for months. He never thought he would use it against Uncle Ivan, but what choice did he have?

This program had many modules, including a video playback subroutine to record and play back video from Tarski's screen, and a sophisticated keylogger. Upon installation, the program notified a server in Yuri's data center that it was active and then periodically polled that server awaiting instructions. Later on, Yuri would instruct his program to copy Uncle Ivan's contacts, emails, and anything else he deemed valuable. He would analyze all of it at his leisure. He would learn Uncle Ivan's secrets.

"Of course you may run your program," said Tarski.

"Excellent."

While Yuri's autorun program silently set up Yuri's special programs in the background, Yuri's fingers flew in a blur across the keyboard and mouse. He visited the website, www.nmap.org and downloaded and installed another piece of software named Nmap. Nmap was the best-known network scanning software in the world. Yuri would install Nmap on this computer and teach Ivan enough about its use to scan the Bullseye network. As far as Ivan could tell, Yuri was installing this software from the memory card, not over the web.

That was the theory—and the riskiest part of his plan. If Ivan caught him in this act, it would be dangerous indeed. Yuri's mother learned this lesson many years ago when Yuri was still a boy, and she taught her son well. She also taught him to be patient and wait for an opportunity to strike. That opportunity was now.

While the software installed on Tarski's computer, Yuri explained the method to learn about this network to which Uncle Ivan was connected.

"If this is indeed a piece of the full network for Bullseye Stores, no doubt you'll want to find its internal database servers. These will lead to your ultimate goal, whatever that is."

"And how do I find database servers?"

"Unlike Hollywood movies, Uncle, one does not sit in front of a terminal and type a simple command to show all database servers. It's never that easy. This task will require a port scan and that's why I'm installing Nmap. Nmap is the best port-scanning tool."

"I'm almost afraid to ask. What's a port scan?"

"It simply means that we are finding out what programs a computer will accept or communicate with."

"Ah—excellent."

"But, Uncle, make no mistake. You're performing a reconnaissance operation, similar to military surveillance in hostile territory. I suggest looking for other routers first to see if they hide from you."

"Hide?"

"Yes. Some routers will stop responding if they sense too many probes."

"More riddles. What are probes?"

"A probe can take many forms. One very basic probe is a program named Ping. Like submarines using sonar, a sending computer sends a ping—an echo-request packet—to another computer. If that other computer responds with an echo reply, you know the other computer is alive. If it does not respond, it may be offline, or something may be blocking your access to it."

"How do I find these other routers?"

"Ping them. But you need to know their IP addresses. Intuition may be the best method to guess their IP addresses. Our default gateway is 10.150.240.1. It seems sensible that other subnets will have similar default gateway addresses and that these will answer pings. Try to ping 10.150.8.1, 10.150.16.1, and so forth until you find a subnet that answers. Then rapidly send, say, fifty or one hundred pings to it and see if it stops responding. If it does, then you know it's sensitive to probes and you must therefore slow down your reconnaissance operation."

"My boy, what you describe is extremely tedious."

"Yes it is. Is the information you seek worth the effort?"

"Yes. It's worth all this effort and more."

"Very well. I'll help you find a few routers in this network and characterize their behavior."

Yuri began pinging IP addresses in sequence as he suggested, starting with the default gateway in this network at 10.150.240.1. It answered the first few and then fifty more without missing any. Next, Yuri tried other possible routers, but nothing answered. He widened his search and started a new sequence of numbers. Nothing answered. He kept changing numbers until 10.100.0.1 answered. So did 10.100.8.1 and 10.100.16.1. Yuri had found some other subnets.

Using multiple windows now, Yuri sent fifty pings to each of these addresses simultaneously. All pings from all addresses answered. Next, Yuri used four windows and sent fifty pings to 10.100.8.1 in each window simultaneously. All answered without interruption.

Routers in this network apparently did not hide when probed.

After satisfying himself that these routers would behave nicely, it was time to try a more aggressive mapping operation. He would first find what was on this private network and then expand outward. He launched Nmap and gave it the appropriate command while explaining his tactics to Ivan.

"This scan will try to identify every system in the subnet. Since nothing hides from us, we will go insanely fast and report verbosely on what ports or programs are listening on each computer. This will take some time to run because it has to scan and report on 2,046 potential computers. Hopefully, nobody will notice our intrusion."

Waiting for this first port scan to finish, Yuri tried again.

"Uncle, we both know you'll be unable to complete your reconnaissance on this network without my help. And the City of St. Petersburg, Russia, has no interest in this specific American retail company. Please do not insult my intelligence. This is your project, not something with the government. Tell me what you're looking for so I can help you find it."

"As I said earlier, I'm not at liberty…"

"Then I can be of no further service to you."

And with that, Yuri stood up and started walking away. "Good night, Uncle. It's late."

"Wait."

"Uncle, I need to get home to my family."

Tarski watched as Yuri made his way out of the study and down the hall. He knew Yuri was right. He would get nowhere with this project without his help. All his years of hard work understanding politics and power would be lost because he lacked the technical know-how Yuri possessed. He was a businessman, not a technician. Technicians, even special nephews, were tools to be used. They were resources, not colleagues. But on this night, he needed Yuri's technology skills. Yuri put on his jacket and reached for the door handle.

"Please wait," Tarski said. "I'll tell you what you want to know. "

Yuri knew now was the time to carry out his mother's wishes.

Yuri turned and faced Ivan. "Why are you practicing reconnaissance on this network? What do you hope to find?"

"I recently found a security software program that tests point-of-sale terminals in retail stores. These POS systems handle money and credit cards and this software tests them for vulnerabilities. I wish to find these POS systems inside Bullseye stores, test them, and report to my superiors. In this way, they will be eager to buy the security protections this software allows and I'll profit from my investment. And I'll share that profit with you because you'll be a key contributor to this project. But first, I need to demonstrate it to dramatic effect."

It was all Yuri could do to keep from openly laughing. Such a ridiculous story. "Ivan must believe I'm still a ten-year-old boy," he thought. "But as Mother taught me, I'll remain outwardly calm and use this to my advantage."

And, adopting the outwardly deferential manner that he had perfected over the years, Yuri said, "Thank you, Uncle, for that explanation. Now I understand what you want. I'll help you."

"Thank you," Tarski said, his usual cocky swagger back in place as he smiled the inward smile of someone skilled in manipulation and deceit.

The port scan finished later that night and showed nothing noteworthy, other than a few Windows servers that might be useful later. That default gateway was an older Cisco router and there were a few other servers in the payment subnet. He could still ping that default gateway even after Nmap subjected it to a high level of traffic.

"Here is how I suggest we proceed. POS systems look like modern-day cash registers. But they are really just computers with devices attached to validate credit cards, hold cash, and track inventory. They cannot operate in isolation. They all depend on one or more database servers. I suggest we start by looking for Microsoft SQL Server database servers."

"What about other database systems?"

"I took the liberty of doing some research. Bullseye is a Microsoft shop with a testimonial on the Microsoft website. They will have a Microsoft database, which is named SQL Server."

"Impressive, my boy! Very well, what's next?"

It was time to hunt for database servers. Yuri explained to Ivan, "We'll scan the entire Bullseye network at a more normal speed. We'll look for port 1433, which is the port on which SQL Server listens. We'll scan the entire network this time, not just this subnet. It'll take several days. I'll check with you in the morning. For now, I really must get home to my own family. And you have Natalya waiting for you."

After Yuri left, Tarski poured a large vodka and retired for the night with Natalya. Perhaps he would buy her a new, imported peignoir the next day to celebrate this success. Maybe not. She had many she had never taken out of the box.

The scan took five days, and each day Tarski called Yuri for an update. The answer was always the same. "Uncle, we are scanning 16,777,216 possible IP addresses. It takes time. Be patient."

When the scan finally finished, Yuri noticed a pattern. There were roughly 2,000 database servers, one in each subnet in this pattern:

```
10.100.0.20
10.100.8.20
10.100.16.20
.
.
.
10.164.48.20
```

"Excellent," Yuri said. "Uncle, do you see the pattern?

"I'm afraid not, my boy."

"Look at the IP addresses. All ending with .20. One database server in each subnet. Around 2,000 subnets with database servers.

Uncle, each of these must be a store subnet. They must keep database servers in each store. If I'm correct, once we know the setup on one store, we will know the setups on all stores. For the next scan, I suggest we pick one of these subnets at random and scan it as we did the ERousseau subnet to see what's in them. Then we can scan a few more to test my hunch."

"Yes, this sounds good."

"Because we will put much traffic through this subnet, we should also start our scan during the American business day so it blends with their normal traffic. And run it even slower to not arouse suspicion."

The scan took fourteen hours. Curiously, Yuri found only a few systems in each subnet in addition to the database servers already identified. Where were the POS systems? He tried several other subnets. All returned similar results.

Bangalore

At Bullseye's remote security-monitoring station in Bangalore, India, recent college graduate Chandra Patel and her coworkers were overseeing all Bullseye network activity in North America. The job was simple enough: watch the network traffic displays and report any unusual traffic that could indicate a security issue.

But determining what was unusual was more art than science. This subnet in Sunnyvale, California, for example, regularly exchanged VPN traffic over the Internet because contractors used it to submit invoices and track payments. Most subnets were in stores. These exchanged encrypted messages with credit-card processors. The sequences were mind-numbingly routine: establish a session, validate a credit card, terminate the session. It repeated millions of times every day.

One spring day in 2013, Chandra noticed a break in the routine when somebody from an IP address in Russia connected to the Sunnyvale subnet. Unusual, indeed—and even more so when that same Sunnyvale subnet pinged and connected to database servers in her store subnets.

As she had been trained, Chandra reported this to the shift supervisor and then prepared a report for the security team in the United States. When her shift ended the next morning, Chandra was proud of herself.

***

Danielle Weyerhauser, an intern with the Bullseye security operations team in Minnesota, found this in her email inbox one morning:

```
From: Chandra Patel
Sent: Thursday, May 02, 2013 2:10 AM
To: SecurityOps@bullseye.local
Cc:
Subject: Unusual behavior subnet 10.150.240.0

Unusual activity detected in subnet
10.150.240.0. Suspected port scan.
Please investigate.
```

"Oh, thrilling," Danielle thought. "How many of these do I see every day?" When she first started her internship in March, she tried to check out every single lead. But each one took way too much time, and each turned out to be a false alarm. It wasn't worth it. She filed this one in her security-incident folder, item number 10,498. "I really should clean that out one of these days."

Thursday, May 2, 2013 was a typical day for Danielle, filled with telephone interruptions for password resets, requests to modify file permissions, and credit-card verification hassles from different stores. She would deposit fifty-seven similar emails into this folder that day, and by the time her shift ended, the unusual activity in subnet 10.150.240.0 would be a blur with all the other unusual activity that happened every day.

More Reconnaissance

After Yuri scanned several subnets over a few weeks and found nothing of interest, Tarski was frustrated. "Where are the POS systems?" he demanded.

"This company's not going to just give us its secrets. But we should have found something by now. Those POS systems probably enabled their firewalls. Let's look for something else."

"Like what?"

"Like the servers that support them. Instead of logging onto a computer, users in a domain log on to their domain. Stores need to operate even if the network connection is down, so they probably have their own domain controllers and DHCP servers."

Tarski was pleased. "So we penetrate these servers…"

"We find the POS systems."

"…And I deploy my GreenPOS program. Okay. Proceed."

"Yes, that's the idea," Yuri explained. "But we need more."

"What more do we need?"

"You'll need to deploy it several thousand times."

Tarski was losing patience, again. "Why so many?"

"You have more than 2,000 stores. If each store has fifteen checkout counters, you have 30,000 POS systems."

Tarski groaned.

"But with that many systems, they must have some automation.

How do they update SKUs? How do they update pricing? When a customer buys an item, how does the system know the cost? There must be a server in each store to update those systems—probably a domain controller. Maybe they interact with those database servers we found and we can use that to our advantage."

"Maybe."

"Probably. But where are you going to store the data, once we get it?"

Tarksi shrugged. "The same server in your data center where we store the lists of websites and users."

"How will you instruct each system to do this?" Yuri shook his head. "And think about thousands of connections simultaneously flowing to Russia. We'll be flooded. We've been lucky so far, but imagine a monitoring system that senses POS systems across the US sending credit-card transaction data to Russia!"

"I hadn't thought about that."

Yuri smiled. "That's why you need me."

"So how will this work?"

"Now that we have port scans of a few of their subnets, we'll look for RDP servers and establish a Remote Desktop session to one of them. We'll find their admin log-in credentials and use those to log on to an RDP server. From there, we'll find a domain controller and see where that leads."

"Admin log-ins? How do we find those?"

"Either brute force or dictionary."

Tarski looked alarmed.

"Don't worry—it's not literal!" Yuri laughed. "They're programs. In a 'brute force' attack, the program tries combinations of letters and numbers until it finds a match. A 'dictionary attack' uses words and variations. But first, let's find the RDP servers. Then we'll crack their passwords."

Yuri entered another Nmap command, looking for RDP servers in each subnet. "This will take several days. Call me when this finishes and we'll take the next steps."

***

As soon as he arrived home, Yuri went to talk with his mother instead of checking in with Oksana, as he usually did. Although disfigured and wheelchair bound, Sofia Makerov's graying blonde hair and tender smile reminded Yuri of his mother's good looks before the car crash.

"Yuri! Why do you come home so late? Oksana became bored and said she was off to visit her mother."

"Her mother's in town?"

"That's what she said."

"Perhaps I should see her, too. But she hasn't returned, even at this late hour?"

"She's an adult."

"I know. I wanted to talk to you about something else. You asked something of me once, many years ago."

"Yes, I remember. It was about that monster, Ivan Tarski, and we haven't spoken of it since. Why do you bring it up now?"

"Because I have something Ivan wants."

"I'm listening."

"I'm working with him on a project that could make a fortune. He needs my computer skills to steal credit-card numbers from millions of Americans. He's blinded by greed and that makes him vulnerable at last. I'm in a position to push Ivan Tarski down to the depths of hell. When that moment comes, I'll take his place. I'll become rich and we'll both dance on his grave."

***

Ivan Tarski knew that sooner or later, Yuri would demand a share of the profits. But these were not profits Tarski wished to share. For now, Yuri was valuable. But soon, Yuri would become a liability and Tarski would have to make some painful choices. But not now. Not yet.

***

The scan for RDP servers finished several days later and Yuri looked over the results. "Interesting," he said. Just like database servers, they also followed a pattern. The 10.100.0 subnet was typical, with systems at 10.100.0.2, 10.100.0.3, 10.100.0.10, and 10.100.0.20, which was also the database server at that site.

"The system at 10.100.0.2 is probably a domain controller and also a DHCP server," he said. "And the entire network is probably a single domain, so if we can penetrate any domain controller, we can control the entire network. And we can install GreenPOS."

"So here's where we guess the password for the administrator account?"

"Yes. With automated tools and some luck."

"There could be millions of combinations!"

"Yes, perhaps billions if they have strong passwords. We'll hope they use a weak password with only a few letters and numbers."

Yuri installed and launched a copy of Ncrack, a program designed to systematically guess passwords.

"This will run for several days, even weeks. Let's hope they don't look at their server logs in this subnet," Yuri said. "And that they keep the default administrator username in place."

"Why's this important?"

"Because if they look at their server logs, they may see failed log-on attempts. Millions of them, until we find the correct password. User 'administrator' is the default name in Windows for the overall system administrator. A best security practice is to set up some other user for administrative functions that require privilege and disable user 'administrator.' For those functions that require the actual name, 'administrator,' temporarily enable it, perform the function, and then disable it. This forces attackers like us to also guess the administrative username, and that makes our attack nearly impossible. But in practice, it's often difficult to disable user 'administrator,' and so we'll hope they didn't disable theirs."

"Ah, very good."

"While we're waiting for Ncrack, we must turn our attention to other phases of the project. We'll extract the credit-card numbers from the POS systems and send those to various servers inside the Bullseye network, which we'll compromise as soon as we have that administrator password. From those internal servers, we'll send the data to other servers across the West, and from those servers, back here to St. Petersburg."

"And why the complicated routing?"

"Because no doubt those POS terminals will be restricted from copying data to external servers. So they'll need to use internal servers. And sooner or later, they'll find out what we're doing and shut us down. When that time comes, we want them to look elsewhere for their attackers."

"Excellent. I like the way you think, my boy."

This was an opportunity Yuri had been waiting for. Ivan would expect Yuri to demand a share of the profits. He would become suspicious if Yuri did not make such a demand. This was the right time to bring it up.

"Uncle, we need to discuss something else."

"Yes?"

"Clearly, you depend on me to execute this attack. Without my help, you won't be successful."

"Yes, I trained you well."

"And you need to share the profit with me. I'm more than an assistant. I'm your partner."

"Partner is it? Partners in an enterprise invest money and assume risk."

"And partners also invest time and possess the required expertise."

"I see. And how do you suggest this proposed partnership work?"

"You and I will share the profits equally."

"You are indeed greedy. Remember, I only wish to inform the people running this company of their security vulnerability. I'm just a humble public servant."

"And I'm just a humble telecommunications analyst. Yet here we are penetrating this American company."

"Never forget that I paid for those skills you possess and I can find many eager telecommunications analysts with your same skills. Yuri, you're a special nephew, but don't think I can't replace you. I won't share the profits equally with you."

"You said you won't share equally. But you don't rule out sharing."

"You're astute."

"You would respect nothing else. Can we agree on 25 percent?"

"Yes. And you've earned my respect."

"Thank you."

"Don't mention it."

"We need to discuss one more topic."

"And what's that?"

"Where's this POS program you purchased, GreenPOS? We need to test it."

"In due time, my boy."

Yuri Makerov and his Uncle Ivan would stay busy while their Ncrack program tried millions and millions of potential passwords, looking for that one combination of letters and numbers that would give them control of the network. It was the last remaining obstacle.

Three FTP Sites

In his years since retiring from the Marine Corps, Tony Harrington had become something of an online gaming expert in his hometown of Indianapolis. At six-foot-five and topping 300 pounds, he liked to tell friends he was a victim of the furniture disease. "That's where your chest falls to your drawers." But at age fifty, Tony still had a full head of brown hair and a youthful twinkle in his eye. To hear Tony tell it, he made the world safe for democracy nearly every night. He also helped many game-software developers pay their college student loans.

His reputation as an authority on the latest in online gaming grew and he taught himself how to program by building his own game, one that he called the ultimate in military simulations. Tony invested in his own server and set up a public FTP site, where he uploaded new versions of his game, incorporating suggestions for improvement and patches contributed by friends, and made them available for free downloads. Maintaining this game served two purposes: it sharpened Tony's programming skills, which would hopefully lead to a better job, and it allowed him to give something back to his online friends.

Tony's FTP site also served another purpose. Because it was wide open to anonymous uploads and downloads, a young telecommunications analyst from St. Petersburg, Russia, named Yuri Makerov eventually found it. Had Tony looked at his FTP logs, he would have found an entry showing a single upload and download from June

2013. This was Yuri's proof of concept while Yuri and his Uncle Ivan waited for their Ncrack attack against Bullseye to finish.

"Excellent," said Yuri to himself. "Exactly what we were looking for."

***

Jennifer Dutcher always enjoyed telling prospective students and their parents how Fool's Gold Academy Charter School of Science and Mineralogy got its name. She pointed to an old, grainy photograph of her great-great grandfather, Donald Dutcher, who came to the Sangre de Cristo Mountains near Santa Fe, New Mexico, in the 1870s to prospect for gold.

After a year of digging, he uncovered a vein of pale brass-yellow colored material while exploring a cave. He should have picked up a sample and brought it into town for examination. But he didn't want to reveal his secret, which would surely attract potential poachers. He bought several dynamite sticks and rented a team of horses and a wagon to extract the minerals from that cave. He eventually dug out two tons of material only to learn it was fool's gold. Every last ounce. All fool's gold. All worthless.

Dutcher's nineteenth century folly became a twenty-first century teaching moment for the school: proper identification is critical! Some of the school projects involved making videos, but the video files were too large to email to teachers. So a parent volunteered to set up an FTP drop-off site, where students could upload videos and teachers could download them. Anybody could use it.

It was the open invitation Yuri Makerov needed. Buried deep in the school's server log was a record of an interaction with an IP address in St. Petersburg, Russia. Another rehearsal so Yuri would be ready when he had the Bullseye password.

***

Frank Langdon Wright's parents were mildly amused when their son decided to become an architect, given that his name was almost identical to the famous Frank Lloyd Wright. But Frank turned his famous name into an asset and built Wright Design into a respected commercial building-design company in Houston. And Frank carried on the family tradition in 1994 when he named his firstborn son Lloyd.

Frank was slow to embrace computers, preferring instead to first do freehand sketches of his buildings. So when commercial customers asked for electronic copies of drawings and spec sheets, Frank turned to Lloyd, now college-age and the family computer expert. Three years earlier, as a junior in high school, Lloyd had proved himself by setting up the Wi-Fi network in the Wright family house. So Frank gave Lloyd the job of setting up the sharing system his customers wanted. Lloyd taught himself enough about servers to set up an FTP site on the company server. Using this FTP site, drafters and designers could save different data sets to the server, and the FTP site would make them available over the Internet for customers and partners. Frank was proud of his son, and had to admit, this new FTP site did make business more convenient. Maybe it was possible to teach new tricks to an old dog after all.

Lloyd consulted community support forums across the Internet and read the warnings about allowing anonymous uploads and downloads. But why make it so complicated? Just teach the designers and clients to talk to each other when a document was ready. Place the document on the site, grab it, and then get rid of it. What could be simpler?

Lloyd didn't need anyone from an expensive IT company to set this up. These guys who called themselves IT consultants were rip-off artists who made things more complicated so they could make more money.

It was a shame Lloyd rejected the warnings he read. It would have saved him a lot of trouble a few months later. And had Lloyd known about FTP server logs, maybe he would have spotted one of the early tests Yuri Makerov executed on his site during the summer of 2013.

The Russians Need a New Approach

Yuri Makerov and Ivan Tarski ran that Ncrack program for more than a month with no results. They also tried other password cracking programs such as Brutus, Hydra, Cain and Abel, John the Ripper, Ophcrack, and several others. None cracked the administrator password. All wasted valuable time.

"Perhaps attacking this problem with technology is the wrong approach," said Ivan. "I suggest a more creative approach might work better."

"What are you thinking?" asked Yuri.

"They'll give us their passwords if they don't know they're doing it. I propose we attack them with email and entice them to visit one of your special websites to install one of your keylogging programs. And then wait for one of them to lead us to the goal. We need a roster of people in their IT department. Bullseye is an American public company. They must publish the name of the leader of their IT department in their annual report on their website."

A few mouse clicks later, Yuri and Tarski learned the name of Bullseye's CIO, Liz Isaacs. The annual report even had a helpful email address.

"How do we craft an email that will pass through the layers of PR departments and make its way directly to her?" Yuri asked.

"Patience, my boy."

Bullseye Office

Danielle Weyerhauser was bored sorting through high volumes of email that wasted her time. The only thing keeping her awake was the steady hip-hop beat pouring out of her ear pods. Her internship was almost over, and now she seriously needed a real job. She loved the people at Bullseye, but if she didn't start working her way up the ladder, she was certain she would go brain-dead from doing so many trivial tasks.

In mid-August, Danielle logged onto her computer and for once found an email with an intriguing message:

```
Dear Ms. Isaacs,

My name is Kachinov Sergei and I bring you
greetings from St. Petersburg, Russia. We are
a poor but proud people and we offer many soft-
ware skills you may find of value. We would be
extremely interested in discussing with you
how we can help augment your team. Perhaps one
day, we may even help open one of your stores
in our city. In my recent visit to the United States, I stopped many times in your stores
and enjoyed the experience immensely. Please
```

```
follow the link to our website below, where we
introduce our team.

Thank you.
Sergei
```

This looked cool. Danielle followed the link to the website and noticed it took unusually long to load. But the website was in Russia, after all, so it probably did take longer to load from that far away. Once the website finally loaded, it looked slick. There were biographies and pictures for about a dozen people and lists of IT buzzwords she had never seen. It even had a video message tailored for Bullseye. When she clicked on it to play, the familiar question came up on the bottom of her browser window:

```
Do you want to run or save MediaPlayer.exe from
Sergei.Kachinov.ru?
```

After she clicked "Run," her screen dimmed and another window popped up:

```
Do you want to allow the following program to
make changes to this computer?
Program name: wmplayer.exe
Verified publisher: Sergei Kachinov
```

"Stop annoying me! Yes, of course! Ughh!"

She clicked "Yes," and finally the video started. It was nice. It showed some guys building a prototype website for Bullseye. There were short scenes of guys brainstorming, typing computer code, testing, and debugging. One of them looked cute. She would have to play this again and see if she could catch his name. The video finished with a picture of a screen showing a nice-looking website with the Bullseye logo in the middle.

Yeah, she would reply to this one and blind-CC Liz. It would take much more than a nice video to give out Liz's private email address. With a blind-CC, Liz would see the message but the original senders would not see Liz's email address.

***

"Sergei Kachinov," a.k.a. Yuri Makerov, smiled as he looked through his email the next day.

```
Mr. Kachinov —

Thank you for your recent communication about
your software development center. Your staff is
impressive! I have forwarded your message to
the appropriate people here at Bullseye. Expect
to hear from us in the next few days.

Thank you,
Danielle Weyerhauser
```

Yuri Makerov also smiled as he watched the web counters tracking access to his newly constructed website increment, one by one. At least five accesses to Yuri's website came from the IP address range registered to Bullseye Stores. "Ivan may not be a technologist and may be a dog," Yuri thought to himself, "but he does know how to manipulate people."

***

The next morning Danielle happened to get into the same elevator as Liz Isaacs, the CIO. A good recommendation from Liz would almost ensure that she'd get a job after her internship was complete, so she wanted to make a good impression.

"Hey Liz, was the email from that Russian programming team something you wanted to see?"

"Hi, Danielle. Yeah, that was great. I forwarded a copy to Ryan and some other people on the IT team. We don't need anyone right now, but their website looks impressive and we might need some talent for projects later on. The video introductions were a nice touch. And they all speak English."

"Thanks, Liz. I can't tell you how thrilled I am to contribute to the department."

"I'll tell your manager you're doing a great job. Why don't you send a follow-up to Russia in a couple days and tell them thanks and that we'll keep their information on file and call them the next time we need outside help on a project."

"Great!"

***

Ryan MacMillan frowned as he opened the latest email from Liz Isaacs: "Ryan, please review the message below from Russia. Take a look at their website and tell me what you think."

"Great," Ryan thought. "Just what I need, a bunch of Russian programmers."

Still, Liz was his boss, so he dutifully opened the Russian website and looked it over. He was impressed, but he didn't want to admit it. This was interesting: they included a video slideshow. He clicked to open it, clicked past all the warnings, and several seconds later, Ryan found himself watching a video of this same group putting together a prototype Bullseye website. "Clever," Ryan thought. He'd have to look more closely later to see if he could spot what tools they were using. He knew he could do better.

"Why was there a UAC warning?" he thought. But before that thought could finish, his cell phone rang.

"Hello, Ryan MacMillan."

"Hey, Ryan, this is Nick on the help desk. I just took a call from the manager at store 227 in Indianapolis. All their checkout systems are locked up. Customers are lining up and nobody knows what to do. Can you take a look at it?"

"Yeah, give me a second. I'm on it."

Looking through his documentation, Ryan quickly found the IP address for that store and started a Remote Desktop session to its local domain controller. He logged in as administrator, gave it the password, and looked at the Event Viewer. Finding nothing unusual, he started another Remote Desktop session to the database server. Looking at the Processes tab of the Task Manager, he found the culprit. For some reason, one of the SQL Server processes on this machine went crazy and was stuck in an infinite loop. With lines of customers backing up in the store, instead of spending more time searching for a root cause, he quickly rebooted the database server. After the fifteen-minute reboot cycle, it appeared to run normally.

He called Nick back. "Hey, Nick, have them try it now. Conference me in."

The store manager's name was Dan King and he was upset.

"Guys, I can't check out anyone right now and I have customers lined up twenty deep in the checkout lines. We're gonna have a riot if we don't get this solved right now."

"I may have some good news," Nick said. "I want you to meet Ryan MacMillan, who oversees all the servers for all stores."

"Ryan, tell me some good news."

"I feel your pain. Try it now. I think you're back up and running. I'm guessing that's what you wanted to hear?"

"Yup."

"After you get everyone moving, I need your help nailing down what happened."

Dan put his phone down and briskly walked out to the store floor, beckoning every employee he could find to stop what they were doing and come help open all unused checkout stations. Then he walked through each checkout line and apologized to customers for the delays as employees logged into their POS terminals and began checking people out. Finally, the store was moving again and Dan figured he could have these lines under control within a few minutes. Now he could go back to the phone to see what else Nick and Ryan wanted.

While Dan worked on reviving the store checkout lines, Ryan scrolled through the event logs on the store database server. He eventually found a series of red-colored event messages starting at 7:03 a.m. that day, indicating some sort of problem with a network interface card.

Dan came back to the phone.

"Guys, we're moving again. Thanks."

"I think I see something," Ryan said. "Tell me what happened around seven this morning?"

"Oh, yeah—there was a lightning storm last night and when I came in this morning, everything in that back room was off. So I turned it all back on and then opened the store. But when we opened at nine, none of the cash registers worked. So I called you guys."

"Okay, that lines up with what I found," said Ryan. "Looks like one of your servers hiccupped when it booted this morning. I'll get some people on the server team to look into it. You should be okay for today."

"Thanks, guys," said Dan.

"If anything goes sideways, call me."

After Ryan hung up the phone, he leaned back in his chair, took a deep breath, and closed his eyes momentarily. Nothing like a good crisis to get the blood pumping.

All thoughts of that Russian video migrated to an out-of-the-way corner of Ryan's mind, where they would lie dormant for several months.

Over four thousand miles away, in St. Petersburg, Yuri Makerov also leaned back in his chair, took a deep breath, and closed his eyes. He was deeply satisfied as his heart pounded in his chest.

The video was Tarski's idea and, Yuri had to admit, it was a good one. When anyone clicked the button to download that video, they also downloaded and installed a special keylogger program that recorded usernames and password fields in log-in screens.

A few seconds after somebody sitting in front of the computer at IP address 10.1.1.25 launched the video player with the hidden keylogger program, that person also logged into Remote Desktop sessions on the servers named indydc227 and indydb227 as username administrator. Yuri's program dutifully captured the usernames and passwords from both sessions and sent them to Yuri's FTP site, where he waited to retrieve them.

It was only a few bits across the Internet. Not enough to trip any alarms. Not enough for anyone to notice. But enough to satisfy Yuri Makerov.

He called Ivan.

"Uncle, the administrator password is 'IheartBulls1.'"

"Wonderful news, my boy. Now come here and let us test it."

One Step Closer

Now sitting in front of Ivan's computer, Yuri could barely control himself as he started the administrator log-in sequence to the domain controller server in his chosen subnet. Clicking the Windows 7 "Start" button, then "All Programs," then "Accessories," and "Remote Desktop Connection," he entered "indydc227.bullseye.local" at the prompt and found himself facing the familiar Windows Server log-in screen. He typed "bullseye.local\adminisstrator" for username and "Iheartbulls1" for a password and waited. When the server responded with "Invalid username or incorrect password," Yuri groaned.

"My boy, look at your spelling of 'administrator'!"

"Ah—yes, of course!"

Yuri fixed his mistake and tried again. This time it worked. They were in. Russian mob boss Ivan Tarski and his prodigy, Yuri Makerov, had complete control over the entire Bullseye IT network from Tarski's home in St. Petersburg, Russia, nine time zones away.

"The first thing we must do is set up our own username and password to make it more difficult to find us," said Yuri.

Yuri launched "Active Directory Users and Computers" and set up a new user named "Best1_User" with full administrative permissions.

"What an odd username," said Tarski. "Why not just pick a person's name?"

"One of the Windows system management companies uses this name. Instead of a person's name, this one will hopefully not arouse suspicion. If anyone does a Google search for this name, they'll find a company named BMC uses it and will be reassured it's part of the BMC product, and safe."

Yuri continued, "Now we must turn our attention to placing your GreenPOS program in all their POS systems. We need to learn how they update their systems with sale prices and promotions, and I have a good idea how they do it."

"My boy, you continue to amaze me. And where will we store all the data we extract?"

"We will find a few internal servers and use them as a temporary repository. Then we will upload that data through the external FTP sites I located, and then download the data here, to Russia. We will be two steps removed from the process."

"You're a genius, my boy!"

"Yes, Uncle, I am. Let me work on setting this up. I'll need a copy of your GreenPOS program very soon. And we need to remove my keylogger program from the Bullseye computers so they do not find it."

"How will you do that?"

"I have a mechanism built in."

Danger

After setting up the Bullseye breach, Yuri spent several days studying the logs from the keylogger program he installed on Tarski's computer. "How ironic," he thought to himself. "I'll use the very tools against Ivan that he uses against Bullseye. Both are equally oblivious."

Yuri grew increasingly frustrated as he found no trace of the GreenPOS program. "Ivan must be keeping it somewhere else."

Ivan did not become a top mob boss by being oblivious. One night after Yuri left, Tarski called his trusted assistant.

"Fyodor, my boy, how is your family?"

"Fine, thanks."

"Ah, good. I called tonight because my computer's acting strangely. I want you to look at it, and perhaps fix it."

"Very well. Shall we say, tomorrow night?"

"Excellent. Thank you."

As Fyodor set his phone on the nightstand, Oksana hit him with a pillow.

"How can you answer your phone when we're in such a romantic setting, my love?" asked Oksana. "That wasn't your wife again, was it? She calls you too often. Why can't she leave us alone? I'm the one you love now, isn't that true?"

"Yes, my love," said Fyodor. "Only this call came from my boss. I'm always on the clock with him. If I don't answer, he'll cut me off, just like that."

"Tarski. What a boor! A wealthy boor, but a boor nonetheless. He has Yuri wrapped up in some big project. He practically drove me to you. Yuri's never at home, and when he is, he's always with his mother. Their relationship is sick. That's why when I come to see you, I always tell Yuri I'm going to see my mother. How can he argue with that?"

"You make me crazy, my clever Oksana. I think of you day and night. It makes me sick to think of you in the arms of that mama's boy."

"I can't wait to leave their apartment and move in with you. Have you told your wife you want a divorce yet? You keep putting it off."

"It's a delicate situation, my dear. Our youngest child's birthday is next week, but I promise I'll tell her the week after that."

"Oh, Fyodor!"

As the two embraced, Fyodor reached over with his right arm and turned off the lamp by the bed.

***

After Yuri left the next night, Tarski called Fyodor, who arrived a few minutes later and started diagnosing Tarski's computer.

"This is interesting. Why does this computer automatically run Notepad when it starts? Very strange."

At that instant, Yuri's cell phone buzzed with a text message. Yuri named his keylogger program "notepad.exe" to camouflage it from snoopers such as Fyodor, and designed it to send an alarm to Yuri if it detected anyone looking for it.

Yuri read the text message and instantly realized he would have no time to waste. He sat at his computer and stealthily connected to Ivan's computer. He watched Fyodor's keystrokes and mouse clicks come ever closer to his program. "This can't be Ivan. He doesn't know how to do these things. Somebody else must be at his computer."

Fyodor said, "Ivan, your computer *is* responding slowly. I'll keep looking."

Yuri sent the command "death" to the keylogger program in Tarski's machine, which prompted it to self-destruct and crash the computer, forcing a clean restart.

Fyodor said, "Ivan, something strange is going on here. Your computer just gave me a Blue Screen of Death and rebooted… Okay … and now it appears to behave normally. Curious, no more reference to Notepad starting up automatically."

***

Yuri talked with his mother the next morning.

"Good morning, my son! What kind words do you have for a broken-down old lady on this wonderful day?"

"Good morning, Mother. You're hardly broken down! I have news. I installed software in Ivan's computer to record everything he's done on it for the past several weeks. He has many online identities and business partners around the world. I saw an email relay service in China, business associates from Iran and Ireland, even a spammer from Florida."

"Why's this important?"

"Because we'll use it against him. But I think Ivan suspects I tampered with his computer."

Sofia's face first turned white with fear, then red as she became angry. Angrier than Yuri had ever seen her.

"What's wrong?" asked Yuri.

"Yuri, listen to me carefully. You put yourself, Oksana, and me in grave danger. These men are criminals and they will murder anyone for money."

"What?"

"See that silver Mercedes parked across the street?"

"Yes, what of it?"

"That car has been there since before I woke up this morning."

"Are you sure?"

"Yes. See the two people in the front seat? The one with the binoculars is watching this building. Yuri, if Ivan finds out you did anything, he *will* murder you. These two may be waiting to kill you right now."

"He can't kill me yet. He needs me to finish the project I told you about earlier. I know how to penetrate that network and access the store-POS systems. I already have everything set up, but Ivan doesn't know that."

"Yuri, you're playing a dangerous game. Don't think he needs you so badly he'll spare you. As soon as you give him what he needs, he'll murder you and I'll lose a son to that monster, just as I lost a husband."

Suddenly, the blood drained from Yuri's face.

"Mother, I gave him the administrator password!"

"What's that?"

"The key to everything. We worked together to find it. And now he has it. He knows the administrator password."

Sofia sat silently for a few seconds, stunned. Gathering her strength, she took a few calming deep breaths, then looked at her son with an icy calm and steel resolve Yuri had never seen from her.

"Yuri, can you work your Internet wonders from anywhere?"

A flash of inspiration hit Yuri as he understood what Sofia was asking.

"Yes. I can access everything I need from anyplace connected to the Internet. All I need is my laptop and some other equipment."

"Go wake Oksana. Pack one of your laptop bags with what you need and an overnight bag. You're taking me to a hotel for the night because I'm upset from spending so much time in this dreary building. After that Mercedes disappears to follow us, Oksana will carry the bags to the Metro station and ride the train to meet us at the Ibis Centre Hotel."

"Mother…"

"Don't question me! I know how these men think. They'll make it look like an accident, just as they did with your father."

"Why the Ibis?"

"Because tourists stay there and we'll be safe. It's also close to the train station. They won't attack at a tourist hotel on a busy street. At least not immediately. And they won't attack on the Metro."

Yuri talked quickly and quietly to Oksana, who became more alarmed each second as Yuri described the situation and what he needed.

"Okay, good. Now help me pack an overnight bag and wheel me to the Metro station. We'll walk past that car as if we have no cares in the world. And while we're walking, we'll only talk about this beautiful day."

After Sofia and Yuri left the flat, Oksana called Fyodor. She saw Fyodor, sitting at the wheel of the Mercedes, answer his cell phone. Who was that big ruffian sitting next to him? She wanted to go over and ask him—and perhaps give him a big sweet kiss, and tell him her special news. But she knew Yuri and his dear mother would be watching. They were always watching. So she put her cell phone on speaker and started packing her overnight bag.

"Did the little boy and his mama leave you behind?" asked Fyodor.

"Stop your nonsense, Fyodor. Why all the big drama? Why are you watching us?"

"I always like to peek through your window, sweetheart. So what's new?"

"I know what's new with me. Fyodor, have you asked your wife for that divorce yet?"

"Sweetheart, I'm sure it'll happen very soon, right after we take care of your 'fiancé,'" Fyodor laughed.

"Listen, we can turn this situation to our advantage if you show a little patience."

"Who, me?"

"Yuri's about to take over Tarski's project—I know that much. If he takes care of Tarski, then that is one less thing for you to worry about. I know how much you hate that old man. What if we let Yuri build up a mountain of rubles before you dispose of him?"

"Now, what would I do with a mountain of rubles?"

"What wouldn't you do? The most important thing is that you marry me and raise our children."

"Children?"

"Work on that divorce, Fyodor!"

***

Safely inside the hotel, Yuri discussed the beginnings of a plan to destroy Tarski by impersonating him on his email accounts.

Oksana asked, "Yuri, how can you impersonate that old wretch?"

Yuri replied, "With email, anyone can impersonate anyone else."

"Won't people be able to spot that?"

"Not easily. Ivan likes to use different email-relay services to keep himself in the background. And he uses different email identities."

"Yuri," said Sofia, "do you have a way to get Ivan's banking passwords?"

"Maybe."

"Turn that 'maybe' into a 'yes' or we all die very soon."

"I know the banks he uses and his bank account numbers—he has accounts in Switzerland, Singapore, and Barbados, but I need to review his computer sessions to search for passwords."

Yuri spent several days playing back Tarski's computer activity. It was tedious and painstaking. And frustrating—every time Tarski accessed his email, Yuri watched him use a stored password so there were no keystrokes to play back.

Yuri found Tarski used six different email identities. One group included Russians named Dmitri Polichev, Grigoriy Lisov, and some others. Polichev looked like some sort of mentor and Lisov was apparently another boss in a nearby city. For these, he was Ivan.Tarski@mail.ru.

Another group included specialists from around the world. An American calling himself Duceml, for example, apparently ran email-phishing campaigns. With this group, Ivan used a variation of his name, ivar2395@mail.ru.

A third group must have been Ivan's investments. These included somebody from Kiev and others. One email exchange with the Ukrainian was a conversation about a program to access memory in POS systems. This must have been Ivan's source for the mysterious program he named GreenPOS—the one Yuri was never able to find. For these, Ivan was Iva0105@gmail.com.

There was a group with a commonality around a website named Linoza.so, which looked like an underground forum for thieves. This website offered all kinds of services, including a marketplace for stolen credit-card numbers. For this group, Ivan used email address Tarman0105@yahoo.com.

A group Yuri categorized as "everyone else" included bankers, real estate brokers, and financial advisors. Ivan used a generic email name with them, ivtar2395@gmail.com.

Finally, Tarski also used his official government email address, I.Tarski@admin.gov.spb.ru, mostly for city business, but occasionally with counterparts in other Russian cities.

A Mercedes parked across from the lobby, and the two men inside it wearing tailored suits became a constant reminder of Tarski, always watching, waiting for his opportunity to strike. No doubt, Tarski also had other men watching the hotel.

Yuri and his family were prisoners. If they tried to escape, all three would disappear on a one-way trip down the River Neva, which ran through St. Petersburg and into the frigid Gulf of Finland.

What time was it anyway? 2:00 a.m. again. What day was this? How many days had they been trapped in this room? Yuri paused the computer session playback, rose from his chair, and stumbled to bed, exhausted. Something about that Linoza.so website. What was it? Thoughts of Somalian domain registrars and images of money changing hands under a table tumbled through Yuri's mind during the few seconds before he fell into a deep sleep.

Three hours later, Yuri woke with a start. Oksana roused. "What is it, Yuri?"

"Probably nothing. Go back to sleep."

"Yuri, I haven't been able to sleep all night. I need to tell you something."

"What?"

"Yuri, are you ready to assume a great responsibility? I hope so, because I learned recently that I'm going to have a baby. I'm pregnant, Yuri, with your child. For his sake, you must beat your uncle and provide for our family!"

Yuri was stunned. He was going to be a father! What would his mother say? She always looked down on Oksana. Maybe out of jealousy of her youth and beauty. But a new grandchild might soften her feelings. How could it not?

"This is great news! I love you so much—and our little one. Please go to sleep now. I may have the solution to our problems."

He kissed Oksana's forehead, and pulled the blanket up tight under her chin. Then he went to his laptop with renewed determination. He was wide-awake. More awake than he had ever been before.

Restarting the playback from a few days ago—there it was—Ivan logged into that Linoza.so website. Yuri didn't notice it earlier because he was focused on email. But there it was: a log-in and a password. Typed on the keyboard this time. What if Ivan used the same password for his email accounts? "Sofia010558." No. This could not be!

Yuri woke his mother, sleeping in the bed next to Yuri and Oksana.

"Mother, in what year were you born?"

"1958; why do you ask?"

"Because you're Ivan's password."

"What?"

"You. And your birthday. You were born on May 1, 1958. Ivan's password to the Linoza.so website is 'Sofia010558.' With a capital 'S.' Maybe this is also his email password."

"Help me out of bed. I need to get up."

Now fully awake, Sofia started some coffee while Yuri quickly launched his web browser, navigated to the mail.ru website, and successfully logged in to Ivan's email accounts. Both Gmail account log-ins were also successful.

"Do these passwords also work for his bank accounts?" asked Sofia.

"Yes! His Achilles' heel. He used the same password for all his accounts. You must have stolen his heart."

"I may have stolen his heart, but he stole your father's life. When I think about that, my blood boils!"

"How could anyone be so evil? Especially to you! ...And me. I swear on my soul, I'll give Ivan's 'love' back to you in full, and by that I mean his money. All of it."

"And to do that, my boy, we must put his soul to rest."

"The world will be better without him. But what you said just now, you said, 'my boy.' That's what Ivan calls me. Funny."

"Don't think anything of it. It's just a figure of speech. To him you're just a way to make more money. That's all he cares about."

"But now we have his passwords. How do we use them?"

"Have you ever heard of Dmitri Polichev?"

"Ivan traded emails with him. Who is he?"

"Polichev is the boss of bosses," explained Sofia. "He's number one in the syndicate of twenty. Ivan is number five. In his day, Dmitri ran all the action in the Soviet Union. The other bosses gave him 10 percent of their profits. Dmitri also maintained order, so minor bosses wouldn't encroach on each other. Those who cooperated stayed alive. He retired to a villa in the south of France, but the syndicate stays loyal to him because he continues to maintain order. Every boss sticks to his own racket, and continues to pay 10 percent to Dmitri."

"How do you know so much about this?"

"I know more than Ivan realizes. All you need to know is your father was number seven."

Yuri was shocked. It was as if he had lived his whole life under an illusion. Nobody was who he always thought they were.

Yuri closed his eyes, looked down, and shook his head. All his life, he had quietly accepted his destiny. A destiny decided by others. The accident, his education, his job. Everything. But no more. That part of his life was over. Now it was time to take fate into his own hands. Past time. He would rid the world of Ivan Tarski by using Ivan's own secrets against him. He would take his rightful place as Ivan's replacement and eventually get rid of all the bosses. Even this Dmitri character. And he would repay his mother for their cruelty.

Yuri opened his eyes and looked up. His facial expression hardened. "What if Ivan emails everyone in this group that he intends to be the new number one? Dmitri and the rest will send Ivan to hell for us."

"No," said Sophia, quietly shaking her head.

"*Why not?*" demanded Yuri, pounding the table.

Oksana woke up and listened to the rest of the conversation, but kept her eyes closed, pretending to still be asleep.

"Because that won't work," said Sophia. "These bosses didn't get where they are by being stupid. They'll know somebody is impersonating Ivan. They might still kill Ivan for his poor security. And then they'll come find you."

"Okay, maybe I'll order a machine gun over the Internet and put some holes in Ivan and his men myself. Yeah, that'll be more fun!" said Yuri.

"No," said Sophia. "There's a better way." Sophia leaned back in her char, deep in thought. "Anton Milekhin," she said softly.

Yuri glared at her. "Who?"

"Anton Milekhin. He also had his eye on me before your father died. He was number eight until they forced him into retirement."

"How?"

"He couldn't control his temper. He made a gesture to Ivan with the middle finger of his left hand. He paid dearly for it."

"What happened?"

"Ivan's security team saw it. They grabbed Anton and contacted Dmitri. Dmitri told them to deal with it as they saw fit. So they cut off Anton's finger and took away most of his territory. A boss never disrespects another boss. That's how Dimitri keeps order."

"Okay. So how does that help us?"

"Grigoriy Lisov. We also need him," said Sophia, still deep in thought.

"And who's he?" asked Yuri.

"Number three. His territory is Veliky Novgorod. I met him a few times. He was handsome when he was younger. And he was good friends with Ivan. He'll do nicely."

"How?" asked Yuri.

"Just do what I tell you," said Sophia.

Manipulating the Mob

To this very day, Anton Milekhin heard stories about the trophy case hanging on the wall in Ivan Tarski's dacha in St. Petersburg; the trophy case holding Anton's left middle finger as the trophy.

The pain when Tarski's men severed Anton's middle finger was all but unbearable. Especially after they poured vodka on the remaining stump to fight infection. The stump eventually healed and the pain subsided but never went away. And since that day, every time Anton looked at his left hand, he went into a quiet rage. Somehow, some way, he would have his revenge.

Perhaps today was that day. After all these years, an email arrived from that scum. "Why does Ivan send me an email?" Anton thought to himself.

```
My Dearest Anton,

As I wander the hallways of my lonely house,
your severed finger haunts me and I wish to
make amends. I have placed $500,000 US dol-
lars in a foreign bank account attached to
your name. Access the bank website at http://
www.bankscott.com. The passcode is the En-
glish phrase "Xtended middle finger". Provide
```

this passcode to the banking authorities and
they will make the funds available to you.
Soon, I'll resign my position with the City
of St. Petersburg and turn myself in to the
St. Petersburg law enforcement authorities,
where I'll provide a complete confession of
my crimes.

Thank you
Ivan

***

Grigoriy Lisov and Ivan Tarski did business occasionally, so Grigoriy was shocked when he read this email from Ivan.

Grigoriy —

I write to you with a heavy heart but I
must unload my burden. So you know this
email really came from me, I remind you of
the oath we both pledged on Saturday, March
14, 1998 with Dmitri Polichev.

It seems Anton Milekhin is up to more trouble. For the past several years, he has
been stealing from our royalty payments to
Dimitri. Working with banking officials to
inflate their money transfer fees, he stole
more than 34 million rubles. We must repay
this debt to Dmitri or suffer the consequences.

If we are unable to repay this debt, I must
resign my position with the City of

```
St. Petersburg and turn myself in to law en-
forcement authorities, where I'll provide a
complete confession of my crimes.

Your brother
Ivan
```

***

"I don't understand," said Yuri. "How will this work against Ivan?"

"Simple," Sophia replied. "I told you only Dmitri Polichev has the power to kill Ivan. But he needs a reason. Ivan was a trusted apprentice and swore a lifetime oath of allegiance. We need to convince Dmitri that Ivan broke that trust."

"But we told Grigoriy—or rather, we said Ivan told him—Anton stole from Dmitri. How does that make Dmitri want to kill Ivan?"

"Both Grigoriy and Anton will speak to Dmitri. Dmitri will check with the banks and find the banks did not inflate any money transfer charges. Anton and Dmitri will also check with the bank to find the deposit date for the money I told you to deposit in Ivan's name. If Anton stole from Dmitri over several years, why deposit the entire amount today? This will persuade Dmitri that Anton is an innocent victim."

"Why steal money from Ivan and give it to Anton?"

"I always felt sorry for Anton. I told you Anton had his eye on me. That was why Anton made that gesture to Ivan. We need to send the money to Anton to make the frame look credible. If we name a phony bank account, it'll look like somebody is framing Ivan. But if money suddenly appears in Anton's name and it's traceable to Ivan, it looks like somebody's framing Anton. Anton will fly into a rage and demand justice, probably with Ivan's middle finger, before Dmitri's men kill Ivan. And Anton will walk away with some money. Small compensation for losing a finger over me. Did you set up that bank account?"

"Yes. Ivan will miss his money soon."

"He'll miss a middle finger before he misses his money."

"What about Grigoriy Lisov?"

"Grigoriy was Ivan's most trusted ally. When Grigoriy and Anton independently contact Dmitri, this will confirm Ivan is framing Anton. And Grigoriy will now help Dmitri kill Ivan, instead of objecting."

Yuri smiled. "You're amazing!"

"Be happy I'm your mother and I love you. You're full of technology wisdom. You need some life wisdom."

A few days later, the evening ferry from St. Petersburg to Helsinki snarled traffic in the Gulf of Finland when it made an unexpected stop less than one kilometer from its departure, after the ferry's second mate noticed a body floating in the water. The captain ordered his ship to stop and sent a lifeboat to retrieve the body. Its forehead bore a bullet hole and its left middle finger was severed. The ship returned to port and left the body with Russian authorities. The body was never positively identified and the murder remained an official mystery, as did the mysterious disappearance of Ivan Tarski. Unofficially, the truth remained a closely guarded secret among a few government officials and others.

Anton Milekhin, living at an undisclosed location somewhere in Russia, keeps his own trophy case in a private room filled with souvenirs and mementos. He added two more trophies shortly after Ivan disappeared. One was a shriveled middle finger that looked more like a bone with skin loosely covering it. The other was a fresh middle finger, mounted in a new frame. Anton vowed he would find a way to preserve it.

Final Preparations

Oksana, Sofia, and Yuri checked out of the Ibis after watching news coverage of the Helsinki ferry incident. The Mercedes was gone. They finally felt safe.

One week later, Yuri visited the administrative office of the City of St. Petersburg. "Is Uncle in?"

"No," said one assistant. "He left here at the end of the business day last Friday and we haven't seen him since then."

"Perhaps he's home sick," Yuri said.

"We tried his cell phone and left voicemails, but nobody returns the calls."

"This is troubling. I'll check on him at his house."

"Thanks."

Yuri's lips formed a small grin as he walked out of the building. But he was careful that nobody saw.

He drove to Tarski's house and walked in the front door, where he met Natalya lugging suitcases across the entryway.

"Natalya, what are you doing?"

"Leaving!"

"Why?"

"Ivan's a pig!"

"Why do you call him that?"

"Several days ago, some men knocked on our door. I answered and they asked for Ivan."

"Who were they?"

"I don't know. One was older, one was missing the middle finger of his left hand. I didn't see the others."

"What happened?"

"Ivan went with them to some business meeting and I haven't seen him since. He's a pig for leaving me here alone over an entire week!"

"You don't know where he went or when he's coming back?"

"No. And I don't care either. I know where he kept his emergency money, and I'm declaring an emergency. Good-bye."

***

Free of Tarski at last, Yuri was unsure what to do next. Walking in a city park with Oksana, he felt the unmistakable autumn chill in the air and noticed the vivid colors of the trees as leaves turned red, brown, and gold. It was mid-October. Snow would come soon and with it, the Christmas season; the time when everyone in the West would use credit cards.

"I'm so close," Yuri said. "I have complete access to their network. But I never found the GreenPOS program Ivan acquired."

"How can you let that stop you?" Oksana asked. "If that old fool could find it, why can't you?"

"You're right, dear Oksana," said Yuri. "It's time for me to act like a man and control my own destiny."

"That'll be the day," thought Oksana, but she said, "I'm proud of you, my darling, and your son is proud of you."

"Yes, and I'll make my mother proud, too."

"Excuse me," said Oksana quickly, "I'm going to be sick."

As she ran behind a bush, Yuri thought it was just morning sickness.

When they returned to their apartment, Yuri went online to methodically search for GreenPOS. He found the developer, a Ukrainian teenager named Alex, and obtained a new copy of the program. Alex bragged that this newer version had updates and bug fixes not available in the earlier version Tarski downloaded. Yuri was so excited he wanted to stand up and scream.

"Mother will be so happy to hear this!" he thought. "I'd better tell her right away!"

He went to the kitchen where his mother was drinking tea and told her the good news. Sofia was troubled.

"Yes, it's good news. But be careful. With Ivan gone, the syndicate will be unstable. Go slowly."

"But I can't wait. Now is the time the Americans use their credit cards. I must strike quickly."

"Your words are filled with reason," said Sofia. "But my heart tells me if you continue with this, you'll die."

Yuri wasn't listening. He was in charge now. And soon, he would join the ranks of the super-rich. As his mother babbled on, Yuri thought about a test run for GreenPOS.

***

Mimi Peterson was a single mom in Carpentersville, Illinois. With Halloween coming, she needed costumes for her two boys, so she stopped at a Bullseye. She found the perfect costumes—really just cheap plastic masks, but she could improvise something to go with them by staining some undershirts with washable dye. When her turn came at the checkout line, she paid with an ATM card. Just another routine transaction in the Bullseye network.

But unknown to Mimi or the store clerks, or anyone other than Yuri Makerov, nine time zones away, this transaction, along with about 2,850 others in the store that day, took a few extra milliseconds to complete. When the store opened that morning, its POS terminals executed the policy Yuri set up to run a script to download and install a copy of the GreenPOS program from one of three internal Bullseye servers normally used for system updates. GreenPOS silently installed, launched, and waited for transactions. With each transaction, it added credit-card information to a temporary file on the POS-system hard drive. At a random time between 10:00 a.m. and 5:00 p.m. US Central Time, it launched a script to add that temporary file to the end of a growing list of credit-card records on one of the update servers. At 7:30 p.m., each intermediate server copied its files to one of the external FTP servers across the United States. One hour later, those external FTP servers downloaded data on nearly 3,000 credit-card numbers to Russia and the welcoming eyes of Yuri Makerov. The first one he examined came from Mimi Peterson.

"Very well, Mimi Peterson from Carpentersville, Illinois," said Yuri. "I won't sell your card number. Not yet. Not until I'm ready."

Yuri built a database to index the card numbers by zip code, significantly increasing their value. Carders would pay a premium because fraud departments would have difficulty spotting phony cards used locally.

By mid-November, Yuri was nearly ready. "The American Thanksgiving holiday is coming," Yuri thought to himself. He sat back in his chair and smiled as he pondered deploying the program at all stores. "Merry Christmas, Bullseye. And Merry Christmas to you, too, Ivan. May you rot in hell."

The Spigot Opens

Yuri and Oksana woke up to a typically foggy late-November Saturday morning in St. Petersburg as icy winds blew sleet and freezing rain. Yuri barely noticed the weather after the full-scale operation he had launched the night before. It was Friday night—Black Friday—in the United States. Yuri checked his collection-server logs from his laptop and found that data on more than three million credit cards poured into his server overnight. He was electrified.

As Oksana stirred in bed, Yuri could barely contain himself. Very soon, they would be rich beyond Yuri's wildest dreams. He would buy boats, luxury cars, a villa in Crimea, and perhaps another villa in Florida or California. Why not a villa in both California and Florida? His mother could have a jet-powered wheelchair if she wanted one, and plenty of servants to satisfy her every whim.

"You appear pleased with yourself this morning," said Oksana.

"Yes," said Yuri. "All night long the goose has been laying golden eggs."

Later that morning, Oksana and Yuri ate a breakfast of coffee, cheese, and sausage. "Soon, we'll have the best beef, pork, and chicken money can buy," said Yuri.

"When can I hold the money in my hand?" asked Oksana.

"Patience," said Yuri. "We're like a farm. Farmers don't get money when they harvest. They have to gather crops into bushels and baskets to sell in the marketplace. Our crop is dumps of credit-card numbers. We'll gather these dumps into collections called bases and sell them in our marketplace. And buyers will pay a premium because our dumps include the US postal code. No one has done that before."

"Where is this marketplace, Yuri?"

"Nowhere," said Yuri with a smile, "and everywhere! It's a virtual marketplace on the Internet. We'll advertise our bases on the Linoza. so website and other forums. We simply post messages about the bases we offer for sale and buyers contact us and pay us."

"How do they pay?"

"Sometimes with wire transfer, sometimes with bitcoin."

"How do we know the buyers will pay?"

"Buyers pay us in advance."

"Why do they trust us?"

"They won't trust us. They'll trust the user named Tarman."

"Tarman?"

"That was the name Ivan used."

"Why use his name?"

"Because Ivan was, or is, a trusted member of this group."

"Huh?"

"This group uses a ranking system based on old Roman names. Ivan carried a rank of Proconsul, which was one of the highest rankings. He probably gave them their seed money for hosting and equipment in return for a share of the profits."

"So you're resurrecting Ivan to sell credit-card information?"

"Yes. But for all the world, Ivan isn't dead. He's only missing, but still very much alive because he continues to access his bank accounts. We have his banking log-in credentials. So we'll impersonate Ivan and sell these credit-card dumps. We'll make hundreds of millions of American dollars. And then Ivan and his money will disappear."

"Hundreds of millions?"

"Or billions of rubles. Or hundreds of millions of euros. We'll probably spread the money among a few currencies. We'll have more money than anyone in St. Petersburg!"

"How's this possible?"

"Oksana, right now, I have three million dumps from only one day of operations. We'll sell each dump for an average price of thirty-five American dollars. Even if we only sell one-third of them, we'll make at least thirty-five million from what we collected just today. Oksana, we have penetrated one of the largest retail organizations in the world. Every time anyone in over 2,000 stores buys anything with any credit card, we'll capture that credit-card number and resell it. By the time this operation finishes, we may have over one billion dollars!"

"Yuri… I do not know what to say!"

"Say you love me."

***

As moderator of the Linoza.so website forum, Fyodor was excited. Dearly departed Ivan Tarski had come back from the grave after two months and was posting credit-card dumps for sale on Linoza.so. Tarski held the rank of Proconsul, so he could, of course, post any advertisements any time he wanted.

Oksana told Fyodor earlier that Yuri was launching the credit-card operation—the mama's boy was hiding behind Tarski's name and reputation to make sales. So be it. Let Yuri pile up the cash, and when the time was right, he'd take it from him. Patience, Fyodor, patience.

Tenderloin

"I'm just a printer trying to earn a living," Abe Garcia told the prospective seller. "That's why I'm interested in this machine."

Cooking smells wafted from dozens of nearby restaurants and apartments in the San Francisco Tenderloin district. Drivers honked their horns in the narrow streets and police sirens wailed in the distance.

Abe was a former sailor with the tattoos to prove it. His current business venture was less honorable but much more profitable.

"Makes no difference to me," said the seller. "$10K cash."

"$10K is a lot of cash!"

"Well, do you want it or not?"

Abe walked around the machine, looking at it from different angles, and then reached to open the cover.

"Hold it right there," said the seller. "If you want to play, you gotta pay."

"Show me a demo."

"It's not my problem if you don't know how to run it. Are you buying or just kicking tires? 'Cuz I have buyers lined up all over town if you're not interested."

"Uh-huh. I can see they're lined up out the door and down the street," Abe said, looking around the empty room. "Looks like the phone's ringing off the hook, too. I'll give you $7,500 for it. $1,000 now, $3,500 when you deliver it and prove it works, and the rest after thirty days."

"You're a thief!" said the seller.

"No, I'm just trying to make a living printing designs on little plastic cards. I want to hear one word from you and that's 'yes.' Anything else and you can sell it to some of these other folks waiting to buy," Abe said, gesturing to the empty room.

"$8,750, take it or walk out the door. Half now."

"How do I know this thing even turns on?"

"Put the money in an escrow account. When I deliver it tomorrow, I'll help you set it up and do your first run with it. When I leave, I have the rest in my pocket. And my next stop is collecting your down payment from the escrow account. You pay the escrow fees. That's the deal. Take it or go back to that Laundromat where you came from."

Abe looked over the machine one more time. Both men knew the ritual. Neither could appear to be too flexible, but Abe needed this machine and the seller needed the money. And Abe and this seller had a long history. Abe knew this was a $12,000 machine and would fit nicely in his shop. Finally, Abe said, "Okay, done. Let's go make an escrow deposit. And I didn't come from a Laundromat."

"Oh yeah? So what do you call a place with a bunch of washing machines where people wash clothes?"

"I call it, 'upstairs.' My shop is downstairs."

"Got an elevator?"

"Why, are your legs messed up?"

"This thing is heavy. I'll need some help getting it in that hole you call an office."

"I have a two-wheeler. And it won't go in my office. It'll go on my factory floor."

"Oh yeah, right. Factory floor. I gotta remember that one. You got power to feed it?"

"Yeah, plenty. Locating under a Laundromat has its advantages."

"So what are you gonna do when everyone uses chip cards?"

"I'll worry about that when it happens. Somebody'll crack the codes and sell chip machines."

The machine installation went well and Abe paid the seller. Another routine transaction. But the seller was right—this shop was getting crowded. Business was booming.

Abe shushed his cat from his chair, sat down in front of his computer, and logged onto Linoza.so. Username: billgates; password: "Micro$0ft!". It was nice play on words, living close to the Golden Gate Bridge. And leave it to a forum for thieves to enforce good password practices. Anyone wanting to know about good website security should look into how crooks secure their own stuff.

Abe was buying today and Linoza.so had plenty of sellers. In Abe's mind, his business was no different than any other. Raw material included plastic card stock and credit-card data. Abe's business added value by reproducing the data onto plastic cards and magnetic strips, and then sold finished products at a profit. And Abe's credit cards looked even better than the originals. Expensive machines and a skilled operator made sure of that.

It was a great business model because the finished products had limited lifetimes and customers had an insatiable demand. The challenge was raw material. Card stock was easy to get, but Abe needed a reliable supply of credit-card numbers. Unfortunately, all his suppliers were crooks and could not be trusted. But the forum moderators knew this, so they set up an escrow system where buyers and sellers could deposit payments into an escrow account until the raw material met expectations. It was a nice system.

What was this? Looks like a user named Tarman was onto something new. With a rank of Proconsul no less. Tarman was offering dumps on a massive scale. And with a bonus—these included the zip codes of the stores where the credit cards came from, so sellers could match potential card buyers with the card zip code to hold off the fraud investigators.

Worth a test. If these worked out, Abe would definitely start buying in bulk. Catch the fish while they're jumping!

Den of Thieves

Gordon Schorr hated his nickname. Shorty. The very word made him mad. Shorty. It started in the third grade as a play on his last name, but now as a high school junior, it was also a description. Barely over five feet tall, with limp light-brown hair covering his ears and bangs over his eyes, it was all he could do to endure two more years at Phoenix Central High School. School sucked. The cheap apartment where they lived on 12th Street sucked. His mom sucked. His dad would also suck if he were still around, but Dad disappeared a few years ago. That sucked. Not having money sucked. Life sucked.

The only thing that didn't suck was the computer in Gordon's bedroom and Linoza.so. The Somalians or the Russians or whoever they were sure knew how to party because this website was awesome. It was filled with smart people from around the world and none of them cared about Gordon's height. Here, he was Lende with the newly acquired rank of Tesserarius. Here, he had respect and even some power because he learned quickly and knew how to do things with computers. He found he had a knack for helping other people with their questions and in return, they helped him with his questions.

He found an interesting post right away.

Billgates: "Having trouble backing up my dumps and other stuff. Takes too long. Anyone got any ideas?"

Billgates was still logged on, so Gordon started a private chat session.

> **Lende:** "Hey Bill, who's running MS if yer here?"
> **Billgates:** "LOL. I'm a different Bill Gates. Big Bill is my uncle."
> **Lende:** "What's a dump?"
> **Billgates:** "Help me back mine up and I'll help you with your question."
> **Lende:** "What the prob?"
> **Billgates:** "I told u. Takes too long."
> **Lende:** "how long?"
> **Billgates:** "About 5 hours"
> **Lende:** "HC—what are you backing up?"
> **Billgates:** "I told u. My dumps."
> **Lende:** "So how big are they?"
> **Billgates:** "About 60GB."
> **Lende:** "What r u backing up 2?"
> **Billgates:** "USB HDD."
> **Lende:** "Looked at USB3?"
> **Billgates:** "What's that?"
> **Lende:** "Lost faster USB2."
> **Lende:** "Woops lots."
> **Billgates:** "How do I get it?"
> **Lende:** "u can probably buy a USB3 card anywhere and put it in your computer."
> **Billgates:** "Not a HW tech."
> **Lende:** "I'll help u."

The conversation went on into the night, ending with Billgates sending "Lende," a.k.a. Gordon, a picture of the insides of his computer. From there, it was easy. Gordon found a PCIe to USB3 adapter with positive online reviews and sent the information and installation steps to Billgates.

And then he went to bed. Another sucky day at sucky school tomorrow.

Three days later, Gordon found a new message waiting for him.

Billgates: "thx Lende U rock! I owe u!"

Gordon smiled. Maybe Billgates was still logged in. Nothing to lose by trying.

Lende: "Ur welcome. What's a dump?"
Billgates: "A dump is all the information in a credit card magnetic strip."
Lende: "How do you get these?"
Billgates: "It's a research project I'm working on."
Lende: "What do you do with them?"
Billgates: "Sell them."
Lende: "Why?"
Billgates: "2 make $$, why else?"
Lende: "No, I mean, what do people do with them?"
Billgates: "Buy stuff."
Lende: "Like with credit cards?"
Billgates: "Tell ya what. Want one?"
Lende: "You mean a credit card?"
Billgates: "Yeah. I'll make u a card to pay u back."
Lende: "Cool. thx."
Billgates: "This stays private, between u and me, K?"
Lende: "K"
Billgates: "Don't spend more than a couple hundred $$. Let me know how it works."
Lende: "Who pays the bills when they come in?"
Billgates: "Let me worry about that. Ur my beta tester. Can I count on u?"
Lende: "Sure."
Billgates: "OK, give me ur address and I'll

send it to u. Remember, keep this quiet."
Lende: "OK"

A week later, as Gordon walked in from school, his mom was waiting with an envelope.

"Gordon, what's this? And who's Lende?"

"Oh cool, thanks Mom! It's for some work I did for a guy."

"What guy?"

"Online. He calls himself Bill Gates, only he's not the real Bill Gates."

"Bill Gates with no return address?"

"I'm going out for a little while, okay?"

"Be back for dinner."

"I'll take my envelope."

"I haven't seen you this happy about anything in a long time. It makes me feel good, 'Lende.'"

"Thanks, Mom. And yeah, that's my new nickname."

Safely outside and alone, Gordon eagerly tore open the envelope. As promised, there was a Visa card and a note from Billgates:

```
Hey Lende — Here is your card, courtesy of John
Riley. Keep it small. Stay under the radar.
Send me a message and let me know how well it
worked.
bg
```

This was so cool—free money! But where to spend it? Gordon left a private message for Billgates.

```
Hey, bg, I was thinking about doing something
online or maybe just doing a cash advance at an
ATM.
```

Later that night, Billgates left a reply:

```
Kid, you need to learn some things. And I like
you so I'll help you get started. Be careful
```

about ordering online because they have to ship it somewhere and you don't want to give anyone your address. If you try to draw cash from an ATM, you'll need a PIN, which we don't have. And even if you did, all those ATMs have video cameras. Unless you want your mug shot all over the news, I suggest you stay away from them. Your best bet is to use the card at a store.

The next day after school Gordon rode his bicycle to the Great Buy store on Camelback Road. He had always wanted a nice Blu-ray player. Maybe there was a way to hook it to his computer and watch movies. Yeah—movies! Sure, why not. He'd get a couple of those too. But how to carry it all on his bike? He would need a backpack—maybe from the Young Navy right next door. Or maybe Great Buy had some backpacks. Gordon chained up his bicycle and walked into the Great Buy store.

"What can I help you find?" asked a store clerk not much older than Gordon.

"Huh? Oh yeah—what's a good Blu-ray player?"

They looked through a few, then Gordon selected one and put it into his shopping cart. Then he wandered over to the movie titles and found two shoot-'em-up movies. And there was a row of backpacks. Gordon selected a nice one. Time for John Riley to spend some money.

Waiting in the checkout line, Gordon's hands started to sweat. His heart pounded. He unloaded the goods and the checkout clerk scanned the items. Total cost with sales tax: $297.53. Now for the moment of truth. He pulled out John Riley's credit card and handed it to the clerk.

Gordon held his breath as the clerk swiped the credit card.

"Sign right here," the clerk said.

"Huh? Oh, yeah, okay."

Gordon started to write the letter *G*, but stopped himself just in time and scrawled an illegible John Riley on the electronic signature pad. He walked out of the store with a new backpack, Blu-ray player, and two awesome movies.

Finally outside the store he could breathe again. He stuffed it all inside the backpack, unchained his bicycle, and started pedaling home.

"Not bad," Gordon thought to himself. "So this is what it's like to be an outlaw."

Gordon got on his computer as soon as he got home and found Billgates online, so he requested a chat.

Billgates: "How did the card work out?"
Lende: "Nice. I have a new blu-ray player."
Billgates: "Great. Now get rid of it."
Lende: "huh?"
Billgates: "If you're smart, you'll sell the blu-ray player and turn it into cash."
Lende: "But I just bought it—it's brand new!"
Billgates: "Yup. And now you'll flip it before somebody traces it back to you."
Lende: "How would anyone do that?"
Billgates: "Think of it as a chain. John Riley will see what you bought. He'll call the bank and cancel his CC. The bank will know where and when you bought it. Two links. Somebody probably saw you walk out of the store with your new stuff. Somebody else probably saw your new stuff where you live. More links. The missing link connects you at the store with where you live. If anyone finds that missing link, you end up as somebody's girlfriend or worse for 5 years. So you pick up the stuff and then flip it fast. And be careful nobody sees you bring it home. Sell it for close to face value so nobody gets sus-

picious. And use different email addresses."
Lende: "This is not easy!"
Billgates: "LOL. If it were easy, everyone would do it. So R U in or out?"
Lende: "I'm in."

The Craigslist ad read, "Brand new blu-ray player with two great movies, all unopened. I don't want it and the store won't take it back. $250." Gordon met the buyer in the Circle K parking lot next to Madison Rose Lane School and walked away with $225 in cash.

"Yeah, Billgates was right. Cash is better." But he kept the backpack.

A few days later, Gordon noticed Billgates online in the Linoza.so forum.

Lende: "Hey Bill. You wanted an update?"
Billgates: "Hey kid—good to hear from you. How'd it go?"
Lende: "Gr8!"
Billgates: "Good job kid. Want some more?"
Lende: "Sure!"
Billgates: "I have a job for you. I need somebody to pick up goods for me. You've proven you can do it. Pick up stuff for me and I'll pay you with your own credit card."
Lende: "Cool, thanks!"
Billgates: "De nada. Just be careful. And don't get caught. I'm counting on you. Do a good job and I'll make sure some of my friends know about you too."
Lende: "Cool!"
Billgates: "So here's how it works. When I need you to do a pickup, I'll send you the name and you put together a disguise. Make sure you look like an adult. Send me a picture and I'll send

you an ID. The store will ask for a picture ID, so that's what you show them."

Lende: "OK."

Billgates: "You need to ship the stuff to me. Keep it for yourself and I'll hunt you down."

Lende: "OK."

Billgates: "I'll set up a bank account with your name. They'll give me an ATM card and I'll send it to you. Use the card to pay for shipping. You pick up the stuff, bring it to UPS or FedEx or the post office, and ship it to me. Pay with the ATM card. Make sense?"

Lende: "Yeah."

Billgates: "Don't use the card for anything else, just shipping. I'll know."

Lende: "OK."

Billgates: "Good. Watch for it in the mail next week."

Over the next two months, Gordon found he had a knack for disguises. Sometimes a young man with a beard and glasses showed up at stores. Other times he was older, with a wig and graying hair. By mid-November, Gordon had around $4,000 in cash and a dozen homemade disguises.

Lende: "Hey bg, now that I have all this cash, what do I do with it?"

Billgates: "Open a bank account. Put the money in the bank little by little so nobody gets suspicious."

Lende: "Sounds like a good idea."

Billgates: "But stay away from credit cards. I hear they're unsafe."

Lende: "LOL."

A vague sense of dread began stirring in the back of Gordon's mind. "I'm helping this guy steal money. And I'm stealing it myself. What happens if something goes wrong?"

A few days after Thanksgiving, Gordon got his answer when "Raymond Cyrus" tried to buy a laptop from Walmart. Gordon swiped the credit card and a few seconds later, the machine displayed one word: "Declined."

"I'm sorry, but your credit card was declined."

"Yeah, I see that. Any idea why?"

"No, I'm sorry. Do you have any other way to pay?"

"Um—no—this is it."

"I'm sorry, sir. Want me to hang onto this while you straighten it out?"

"Yeah, thanks."

Gordon's heart pounded as he left the store, empty handed. But no police followed, no lights, no sirens, nobody brought him downtown for questioning. "I watch too many old cop movies," he thought. He hopped on his bicycle and pedaled home. The air felt chilly.

```
Lende: "Hey bg, that CC was declined. Never
happened b4."
Billgates: "Sorry kid. It happens. Sometimes
the CCs are from another part of the country
and the processors decline them. I'll send you
another one. I have a sweet base here that even
has zip codes. I'll make sure to send one from
somebody near you."
Lende: "Thanks."
```

Billgates kept his word and two days later, a new card arrived in the mail. Gordon opened the envelope and looked at the new card. His jaw dropped. The name on the card was Michelle T. Schorr. That was his mom! Michelle Tina Schorr. OMG!

First Alerts

Monday, December 9, 2013

"Hey, Brenda, come take a look at this." Jesse Jonsen and Brenda Yang worked in a hot, cramped basement office where the Uncle Sam Bank antifraud group operated. Jesse was a whirlwind of activity and one of the most committed fraud fighters in the banking industry. People underestimated Jesse at their peril.

Brenda was in her mid-forties with black hair. Taller than Jesse, she rounded out the team. What Brenda lacked in energy, Jesse contributed. And what Jesse lacked in experience and wisdom, Brenda provided. They were a good team.

It was a typical early December morning in downtown Minneapolis, with the outside temperature well below freezing. But inside this basement office, the temperature hovered in the mid-eighties as heat from network equipment and dozens of computers overwhelmed an air conditioning system designed for an earlier era. "And happy Monday morning. You're not gonna believe this."

Brenda took off her coat and looked over Jesse's shoulder as Jesse clicked mouse buttons on her computer.

"I was looking at these new bases for sale on Linoza.so and noticed this huge one this morning."

"Oh, wow!"

"Five million dumps?"

"Yeah, and that's just from Friday. I haven't looked at Saturday and Sunday yet."

"We should look at the BINs."

"I was thinking the same thing."

Jesse clicked some more mouse buttons and brought up a list of Bank Identifying Numbers in this batch of credit-card numbers, sorted in ascending order. Jesse and Brenda both started scanning. Thirty minutes later, they met with Lynn Northrup, the department manager, in a fifth floor conference room. Lynn was African-American and, like Brenda, also in her mid-forties.

"Let me get this straight," Lynn said. "You found five million new credit-card numbers up for sale this morning and more than a hundred-thousand of them are from our bank?"

"That's right," said Brenda. "Looks like the Russians were busy overnight."

"Okay," said Lynn. "Contact Visa. Share what you found and ask them to put an alert on anything with the BINs you uncovered. How much do these guys want for a dump?"

"Thirty-five dollars," said Jesse.

"Premium priced, huh?" said Lynn.

"These have zip codes," said Jesse.

"What?" asked Lynn incredulously. Brenda also raised an eyebrow.

"They have zip codes," repeated Jesse. "I'm not sure whose zip code yet, but these dumps come with zip codes. That's why they're more expensive."

"Hmmm. That does make things interesting," said Lynn. "Okay, buy one hundred of them. Brenda, you're the credit-card expert. Do you think that's a big enough sample?"

"Yeah, that should do it for now," said Brenda. "We'll need more later on, especially when the next wave comes in."

"You think there will be more?" asked Lynn.

"I'd bet on it," said Brenda. "Somebody found a gaping hole and they're just getting started. I'll analyze what's in common with the hundred we buy. I should have an answer before lunch."

"Okay. I'll alert upstairs," said Lynn. "Brenda, would you also call MasterCard, Discover, and Amex and alert them as a courtesy?"

Two hours later, the next meeting was in a conference room on the twentieth floor, with Jesse, Brenda, Lynn, and Harlan Phillips, director of credit card operations. Harlan was bald on top, overweight, and always wore a white dress shirt with rolled up sleeves and a loosened tie. Senior Vice President of Operations Mike Swanson was on a speakerphone from a Florida golf course.

"My one vacation week," laughed Mike.

"You can run but you can't hide," said Lynn. "Let's get to it. Brenda, what do you and Jesse have so far?"

"We bought the hundred cards, but it was a process," said Brenda. "Jesse noticed that zip code and our friend, Tarman, was charging a premium. So we figured we'd try to negotiate."

"Wait a minute," said Mike. "We're buying fake credit cards from crooks?"

"Yeah, I guess technically we are," said Jesse. "Unless you have a better way to find out what we need to find out. But as far as anyone in the Linoza.so world knows, Teena Fay from Green Bay is the real buyer. She has a rank of Legionaries. She has a Gmail email account and her spelling and grammar are awful."

"Legionaries?" asked Harlan.

"It's a long story," said Jesse. "Essentially, these guys rank their members based on reputation. And they use old Roman names. All part of the mystique I guess."

"It's all Greek to me. So bring me up to speed," said Mike. "Somebody has five *million* credit-card numbers up for sale? And of that five million, one hundred-thousand are ours?"

"Well, um, no," said Brenda.

Jesse took over. "We've learned more since this morning. Now we think about one million of those are ours. So far. And the total number including Saturday and Sunday is something like fifteen million. And climbing."

Nobody said a word for about thirty seconds as the news sunk in. Everyone did the calculations in their heads. With one million credit-card numbers compromised and an average credit limit of $2,000, the potential liability was significant.

Jesse continued. "My alter ego, Teena, got Tarman to provide a list of BINs.

"Tarman?" said Harlan.

"He's the guy selling the cards. Teena told him there are a few BINs she likes and she might want a hundred or so if the right BINs are in the mix. That makes it worth his while to give us a little customer service."

"A nice, user-friendly criminal website," commented Harlan.

"Anyway," continued Jesse, "we loaded the BINs he gave us into a CSV file and sorted in ascending order and compared our master list of BINs with the BINs up for sale. Twenty of the BINs were ours. Tarman provided a count of each BIN. Ours added up to about one million. Something like 1,000,104, something like that. I can show you the chat log on the projector if you want. Mike, I'll email it to you."

Mike said, "No, you don't need to do that."

"I bought one hundred cards," said Jesse, "and then Brenda and I did our commonality analysis."

"And?" said Lynn.

"They all have one merchant in common," said Brenda. "Bullseye."

Harlan and Lynn leaned back in their chairs and pondered what Brenda had told them. Finally, Mike broke the silence over the speakerphone. "I didn't want to spend a week in Florida in December that badly anyway."

Everyone laughed nervously.

Harlan said, "So, you're coming home tomorrow?"

"With two billion dollars in potential liability, yeah, I'll either get on a flight tonight or in the morning," said Mike.

"We should call law enforcement," said Lynn.

"I'll put in a call to the FBI right away," said Harlan. "And when they ask me why we're buying back our own stolen credit cards and putting money in this guy's pocket, what do I tell them?"

"Tell them we bought back one hundred cards out of one million of ours up for sale," said Brenda, "because that's the only way we have to find out where they came from."

"And what's the deal with the zip codes?" asked Harlan.

"We're still not sure," said Brenda. "We don't think they're the cardholder zip codes because how would that get into a dump? It's not on the magnetic strip. They aren't the issuing bank's zip codes because that's us and I did a quick scan of some of the zip codes from the cards Jesse bought and we don't have branches in some of them. So that leaves the acquiring banks and the merchants. If I had to bet, my money would be on the merchants."

Over the speakerphone, Mike said, "Wait a minute—I walk into a Bullseye, buy something with a credit card, and after a while, my credit-card number and the store zip code shows up in this guy's inbox?"

"Yeah, that pretty much sums up what we know now," said Brenda.

***

Chandra Patel was mystified as security-event notifications flooded her monitors and those of her teammates in the Bangalore security operations center. Why were Bullseye POS terminals in Sunnyvale, the location Chandra monitored, and others across the United States suddenly sending uploads to a corporate update server? What were they uploading?

Chandra followed the procedure on her well-worn incident response flowchart and sent her required email to the security team in Minneapolis, hoping somebody would answer this time. As did the sixty other people working this shift in the security center who saw the same thing.

"Karnesh, you need to see this," said Chandra to her supervisor.

Karnesh Kumar was a seasoned IT expert and helped sell this center's service to Bullseye. The deep lines in his face told a story of years of hard work, and his wide smile telegraphed appreciation for the large customer he was able to attract. He still carried vivid memories of frigid Minnesota winter weather from his trips to the US to meet with Bullseye IT staff.

Karnesh walked past the rows of people, computers, and monitors, and watched with alarm as monitoring station after monitoring station reported the same thing. Sunnyvale, Denver, Boise, Des Moines, Omaha, Dallas, Indianapolis, Cleveland, Boston, everywhere. The monitoring stations for every region showed the same thing. POS terminals from every store were periodically sending traffic to one of three corporate update servers.

"I see it," said Karnesh. Playing a hunch, he sat in front of a computer and queried the external traffic log from the previous day, looking for matches to the IP addresses belonging to those update servers. Next, he eliminated external IP addresses registered to Microsoft and other possible update sources. He was shocked to find a nightly FTP upload from each of those update servers to one of three unknown external FTP servers. "Let's do a Whois lookup and find out who owns those external FTP server IP addresses. What do they have in common?"

Chandra spoke up a few minutes later. "I have the results. One is from a school in New Mexico, one is from Houston, and the third is from Indianapolis. Why would Bullseye send FTP uploads to these places?"

"An excellent question," Karnesh replied. "And one I'll immediately ask."

The email was short and to the point.

```
From: Karnesh Kumar
Sent: Wednesday, December 04, 2013 9:08 AM
To: Ryan MacMillan
Cc: Liz Isaacs
Subject: Alarming traffic to 3 FTP sites

We have detected uncategorized software on
three internal servers and an alarming flow of
FTP traffic from them, terminating at three dif-
ferent sites. One site is in New Mexico, one in
Indianapolis, one in Houston, Texas. Are these
FTP uploads something we should expect to see?

Regards,
Karnesh
```

"Surely the managers at Bullseye will be pleased with us," Karnesh thought to himself. He was proud of his team and hoped to grow this security center. Many families depended on the income it generated. He would not let his employer or customers down.

***

If only the Bullseye managers had seen Karnesh's email, or any of the dozens of alerts sent by the monitoring staff in Bangalore. Although the security operations team had twenty people in Minnesota, Danielle Weyerhauser, an intern, was the only member of the SecurityOps email group and she left the company in October. The Bullseye HR department followed all the proper policies and procedures when Danielle left, and the IT department disabled her account, subject to deletion when her line manager gave the okay and submitted a help desk ticket, which would require the appropriate signatures. Unfortunately, it was on nobody's flowchart to add anyone else to the SecurityOps email group. So nobody saw the emails from Bangalore because nobody was assigned to check them.

Shortly after signing the agreement with Bangalore, Ryan MacMillan set up an Outlook folder named "Bangalore" and a rule moving all emails from the people in India into the Bangalore folder. A few days after setting up that folder, Ryan forgot all about it. So he also missed the follow-up emails from Karnesh, including this one:

From: Karnesh Kumar
Sent: Monday, December 09, 2013 6:04 AM
To: Ryan MacMillan
Cc: Liz Isaacs
Subject: RE: alarming traffic to 3 FTP sites

The traffic to the FTP sites mentioned last week seems to follow a pattern. Each of three internal servers sends a burst to one of the external sites each day. We are still working to understand this traffic. What is special about New Mexico, Indianapolis, and Houston, Texas?

Please advise. Is this something we should expect to see?

Regards,
Karnesh

Liz Isaacs' Out of Office Autoreply summed up her status:

From: Liz Isaacs
Sent: Wednesday, December 04, 2013 7:39 PM
To: Karnesh Kumar
Subject: Out of office autoreply

Thank you for contacting me. I am out of the office until Monday, December 9 speaking at a retail technology conference and will not have easy access to email. If this is urgent, please direct all inquiries to Ryan MacMillan, Director of Server Operations.

Regards,
Liz

Regina

Even after escaping a lifetime of abuse in Guatemala and eighteen months living in a Laredo, Texas homeless shelter, Regina Lopez still looked radiant and maintained a quiet inner dignity with her shoulder length black hair and disarming smile. She wiped her daughter's face with the cleanest washcloth she could find. The shelter staff tried to provide clean towels, washcloths, soap, and hot meals, but it was a struggle because there were always too many people and not enough supplies to go around. They were decent and caring, but Regina felt an underlying tension because they were overwhelmed. Her new country was not as rich as the mules promised.

The shelter filled up every night; every morning, men from the INS took many new arrivals four blocks south and three blocks west to the Convent Avenue Port of Entry and dropped them on the Mexican side of the border. But not Regina and her daughter. Juanita was an American citizen and the INS could never send either of them away. It was a miracle.

The United States really was the land of opportunity, although as far as Regina could tell, the streets—at least those that she could see near the Hidalgo Shelter—were paved with dusty, clay bricks and asphalt, not gold. Barely literate in Spanish, her challenges as a homeless single mother in a new country were daunting. But with help from many people, she made remarkable progress and by now she could speak rudimentary English and read at a fourth-grade level.

And it was time for another miracle because the maximum time anyone could stay at the shelter was eighteen months. But Regina was prepared and the shelter staff worked with her on a plan. As the mother of an American citizen, she was entitled to a cash-assistance card to help with food and clothing for the baby. The shelter staff taught Regina how to set money aside to accumulate enough for a deposit on an apartment; by now she had enough to cover the deposit on a moderate apartment, plus a little extra.

The next miracle was finding a way to generate enough income to pay rent every month. The cash-assistance card was not enough. And that led to today, Monday, when she was scheduled to meet with the managers at the Rial Laredo Hotel at 9:00 a.m. sharp about a new job cleaning rooms. It was a big day and the shelter staff had hovered over Regina all Sunday and early Monday morning, fixing her hair, applying makeup, grilling her with practice interview questions and evaluating her answers. Finally, she was ready.

The five-block walk went quickly and the interview was flawless. The manager offered her the job on the spot. Her first day would be next Monday, one week away.

Regina was ecstatic. "Oh Lord, thank you for your generosity. Thank you for life in this wonderful country. We are blessed beyond measure with your kindness."

Back at the shelter, Regina reported her good news. Amid all the poverty and heartbreak from across the border, this was sweet victory and time to celebrate. They needed a reminder of this wonderful day, so they drove to the nearest Bullseye, where Regina bought Juanita a special Christmas gift. It was a snow globe, showing a castle surrounded by a winter landscape. No matter how cloudy and snowy, the castle representing her new country would always be strong. The clouds would always part as the snow stopped falling, and the day would turn out clear and bright. It was a beautiful symbol and Regina could not think of a better way to celebrate with her new American friends.

Regina's friends offered to pay, but Regina insisted on paying the $13.99 herself. Regina knew the money attached to her cash-assistance Visa debit card was a grant from the government, but using the card gave her a feeling of independence. This was a special occasion and a new beginning—her first purchase beyond basic food and clothing in her new country. Besides, the card had plenty of money to make the upcoming apartment deposit and first month's rent, with a little bit left over for emergencies. With her new job, soon she would not need this card anymore. She would pay back her new American friends who helped her and would remain friends forever.

After buying the gift, Regina and her friends splurged at a nearby McFrank's. They were overjoyed when Juanita ate nearly all of her hamburger. Juanita allowed her mom to share the French fries and lemonade, and the whole group shared a toast with soft drinks. Everyone had a wonderful time. Regina was on her way to self-sufficiency and this would be a success story for the shelter.

By the time the group returned to the shelter Monday night, a copy of Regina's debit-card number was already in a database on a server in St. Petersburg. Later that night, a counterfeiter with a shop below a Laundromat in San Francisco's Tenderloin neighborhood bought the card number from an underground website and printed a forged Visa card embossed with Regina's name and credit-card number. On Thursday, an anonymous thief in San Antonio used the card to buy a laptop computer and gaming software for $726.53, leaving a balance on the card of $3.47.

On Friday morning, Regina met with the landlord to finalize the details. She would move in over the weekend and start work on

Monday. The apartment was within walking distance from both the Rial Laredo and the shelter. Friends on the shelter staff agreed to watch Juanita during the day while Regina worked, which meant Regina could see her over her lunch break. This stretched the shelter rules, but the shelter managers okayed the arrangement because this would be the success story the shelter needed to continue receiving grants. If anyone deserved a break, it was Regina, the model client.

"Just one more detail to take care of," said the landlord. "I need to run your card."

Regina handed her Visa card to the landlord. He swiped it through the credit-card machine.

"Please wait... *Declined*. Insufficient funds," it read.

"Um, Regina, there seems to be a problem. I thought you said you had plenty of money on this card."

"I do. What is wrong?"

"Well, the machine here says you don't."

"What means 'insufficient funds'?"

"It means you don't have enough money on the card to cover your deposit and first month's rent."

"How can this be? I save my money. Statements in the mail say I have enough money."

"I don't know what to tell you. This machine says you don't have enough."

"Then machine is wrong. Here—phone number on the back of card. We call."

The landlord grudgingly handed Regina his cell phone. "They always have plenty of money until it's time to pay up," he thought. "Why do I keep letting that shelter con me?"

Regina's hands shook as she dialed the phone. She had almost $800. How could she not have enough money?

"Press 1 for English, presione 2 para español," said the interactive voice system that answered the phone.

She pressed 1.

"Please enter your sixteen-digit account number followed by the pound sign."

"What is pound sign?" asked Regina. The landlord showed her the "#" button on the phone. Regina started pressing digits, but made a mistake.

"I'm sorry, but you have entered an incorrect account number. Please re-enter your sixteen-digit account number, followed by the pound sign."

Regina carefully entered her account number, but the system timed out before she could finish. As she was about to enter the thirteenth digit, the automated voice said, "Thank you for calling EBT payments. Good-bye."

The landlord pressed the "Speaker" button on the cell phone and helped Regina dial the number again. This time, they made it past the account number entry.

"Please enter the last four digits of your Social Security number," said the voice. Regina found her new Social Security card—the staff at the shelter told her not to lose this—and pressed the digits on the phone.

"Press 1 for balance lookup. Press 2 for recent transactions. Press 3 to report a lost or stolen card. Press 9 for an operator," said the voice.

Regina pressed 1.

"Your balance," said the voice, now becoming monotone, "is three dollars and forty-seven cents."

"How can this be?" asked Regina.

"I'm sorry, but I do not recognize that command," said the voice.

"I have almost $800!" said Regina. "I save every month since Juanita born!"

"I'm sorry, but I do not recognize that command," said the voice. "Press 1 for balance inquiry. Press 2 for recent transactions. Press 3 to report a lost or stolen card. Press 9 for an operator."

The landlord said, "Try pressing 2."

Regina pressed 2, and the voice said, "Here are your transactions from the past seven days. On Thursday, December 5, you purchased a computer from Great Buy Company in San Antonio, Texas. On Thursday, December 5, you purchased software from Great Buy Company in San Antonio, Texas. On Thursday December 5, you purchased software from Great Buy Company in San Antonio, Texas. On Thursday, December 5, you purchased software from Great Buy Company in San Antonio, Texas. On Thursday, December 5, you purchased software from Great Buy Company in San Antonio, Texas. On Monday, December 2, you purchased a household item from Bullseye Stores in Laredo, Texas."

"I did not buy those things in San Antonio!" cried Regina, now nearly hysterical.

"I'm sorry, but I do not recognize that command," said the voice. "Press 1 for balance inquiry. Press 2 for recent transactions. Press 3 to report a lost or stolen card. Press 9 for an operator."

"My card right here. It not lost or stolen!" said Regina. "I not buy these things!"

"I'm sorry, but I do not recognize that command," said the voice. "Press 1 for balance inquiry. Press 2 for recent transactions. Press 3 to report a lost or stolen card. Press 9 for an operator."

The landlord said, "Let's get somebody to talk to us," as he gently took the phone from Regina. He pressed 9.

"Transferring to an operator. Please wait while we handle an unusually large call volume today," said the voice. A 1970s-era easy-listening rock song started playing.

Regina and the landlord listened to easy-listening rock songs for the next forty minutes as they waited on hold. Suddenly the music stopped and they heard the sound of a ringing phone. After six rings, the connection dropped as the automated phone system on the other end of a toll-free phone number hung up.

The landlord looked at his phone, swore under his breath, and said, "Wait a minute. The battery's almost dead. Let me get a charger."

Fifteen minutes later, with the phone now connected to a battery charger, they tried the call again. This time the landlord pressed 9 immediately after entering Regina's account number and other required numbers. Regina sobbed as they waited another forty-five minutes listening to cheerful songs from the Captain & Tennille. But this time, somebody answered when the phone rang.

"Hello, my name's Belinda, how may I help you?" said a cheerful voice with a slight southern accent.

"Hi. I'm with Regina Lopez here and we seem to have a problem with her Visa card."

"Okay. What's the account number, please?"

"Didn't we enter that on the phone about an hour ago?" said the landlord.

"You probably did, but I need it now," said Belinda.

Regina read her the account number and the last four digits of her Social Security number. She had to do it three times because static in the call and Regina's accent made understanding more difficult.

"I see your last few transactions," said Belinda. "Looks like you bought a computer and some software."

"Yes, in San Antonio," said the landlord.

"But I have never been there," said Regina. "I'm in Laredo, Texas, in the United States."

"I see," said Belinda. "Perhaps you ordered these over the phone or over the Internet? The stores might not show up in the same city where you live."

"I did not buy these things!" said Regina, emotion rising in her voice. "I need this money for my apartment. I did not buy these things!"

"Perhaps you loaned your card to somebody?" said Belinda.

"I keep my card with me in my purse all the time," said Regina, "just as they teach me. I save money for this day to move into an apartment. I buy present for my baby, Juanita, on Monday. I not buy nothing in San Antonio!"

"Our records indicate you bought a computer and some software from a Great Buy store in San Antonio last night. But you're saying you did not buy those things?" said Belinda.

"That's right," said Regina. "I buy Christmas present for Juanita, my daughter on Monday. I not use card other than that. Your record's wrong!"

"We can investigate this further. We should also cancel this card and issue you another one. It should arrive in the mail in about a week," said Belinda.

"Thank you, but can I pay landlord with new card now? I'm supposed to move in over this weekend and I have nowhere else to live and no other money."

"Ms. Lopez, I'm truly sorry, but the new card will have the same $3.47 balance as the old card. We cannot add more money to the card balance."

"But I did not spend that money!"

"I understand, but I cannot replace the money that was taken from the card. Perhaps you should call law enforcement and report this. Maybe they can recover some of it for you."

The call ended a few minutes later with Regina in tears. And then it got worse.

"Regina, I'm sorry, but I can't rent to you if you don't have the money to pay," said the landlord. "I have at least a dozen people waiting for this apartment who can move in tomorrow. I put you at the front of the line because they asked me for a favor at the shelter, but if you don't have the money, I need to let somebody else have it."

"But where will my daughter and I live?" cried Regina.

"I don't know what to tell you. But if I were you, I'd call the police."

***

"What do you mean, declined?" asked KLRD TV News Director Luis Granados to the restaurant cashier. Tall and slender, only his graying hair gave away his late-forties age. In the TV business where youth sells, Luis knew he could dye his hair to look younger, but his job was behind the cameras and the "experienced" look gave him an aura of authority at the station. So he left his hair its natural gray. "The only time I used that card was the other day at Bullseye. I can't be over my limit, unless the limit's about twenty dollars."

"I'm sorry, sir, the machine doesn't say why, only that it was declined."

"Here, I'll take care of it," said junior reporter Carlos Cardenas. Carlos looked like a younger version of Luis, only shorter and heavier and with a TV face that subtly said, "You can trust me." "How often does a reporter get a chance to take the boss out for lunch?"

"Okay, kid, thanks. Put it on your expense report. I'll approve it. And I'll get to the bottom of this credit-card problem when I get back to the office."

"Thanks for the great job review by the way," said Carlos as he paid the bill with his credit card. "I like working here. Maybe I'll do a story about credit-card fraud right here in Laredo. Want to be an interviewee? We can place the camera over here on your good side."

"Very funny. I have something else in mind for you. We do murder and mayhem stories every night. But now it's Christmas and everyone wants a feel good story. You're going to find me one."

"How will I do that?"

"Use your imagination. But here's where to start. Your parents and my parents immigrated to this country. We're American citizens. But now there are thousands more like our parents crossing the border. Some legal, some not. One of those people has a story worth telling. Go find it. Start at that shelter on Hidalgo and see what you can turn up. Put tears in my wife's eyes."

"What, no tears in your eyes?"

"When our ratings go up by 5 percent, then you might see tears in my eyes."

"Okay. I'll pick up my car at the office and head over there."

"No. I don't want to see you again until you get me a great story."

"But we rode here together in your car."

"Yup. And now you're taking the bus from here to that shelter. Get a receipt and put the bus fare on your expense report. When you're ready for footage, call the station and I'll send a camera crew out. I want that story for Sunday night. That gives you forty-eight hours for raw material so we can edit it in time for the 10:00 p.m. show. Why are you still standing here?"

Forty-five minutes later, Carlos shared an El Metro bus with an immigrant family, an older man with a bushy beard who needed a bath, a few people dressed in suits headed downtown, and several teenagers laughing with each other over a cell phone video. Carlos barely noticed the people around him as he called the research department at the station to find out all he could about this shelter in the next few minutes.

"Congratulations, kid, when the old man sends you out for a story like this, it means he likes you," said the station research director.

The bus ride to the stop nearest the shelter only took fifteen minutes, but it was enough time for Carlos to come up with an approach.

The faded tan-and-aqua-painted brick building looked as inviting as the staff could make it, which was not much. A barred security gate covering a closed side door was locked tight. The building was on a corner, but had no windows facing either street. The main entry door on a corner of the building was unlocked, with a barred security gate in front of the door to keep intruders out when the building closed. But in a gesture that looked almost like an apology for the secure door, somebody had wrapped the bars on the gate with a red Christmas garland.

Carlos walked in and blinked for a few seconds as his eyes adjusted from the bright light outside to the dark inside. He saw a few tables in a community dining room with a stainless steel counter and serving window at the back. Behind the counters was a kitchen with a few people cleaning up. The tables were empty. Some people stacked chairs, others wiped down tables. Carlos noticed a group sweeping, while one person started mopping in another corner of the room.

A staff member in her early twenties approached Carlos. "I'm sorry, but we just finished up lunch. If you're hungry, stick around and we'll have dinner at five."

"Thanks," said Carlos. "But I'm not hungry right now. I'm Carlos Cardenas from KLRD and I'm hoping to do a story on the work you do."

"Oh! Well in that case, let me introduce you around! Is this, like, a real TV story?"

"Yup. My boss wants to run it Sunday night."

At that moment, Regina Lopez burst in, trying but failing to hold back tears. She walked to a table with some chairs that had not yet been stacked, slumped down on one, put her head on the table, and started sobbing.

"Excuse me for a second," said the staff member. "Regina, honey, what's wrong?"

"My... my cash card. Empty! I cannot pay landlord because my cash card is empty!"

"Wait a minute. Regina, that can't be right!"

Carlos wandered over. "I'm sorry, I couldn't help but overhear. What happened to your cash card?"

The staff member interjected. "Look, Mr.—um—Cardenas, maybe this isn't a good time for a TV story right now. Can you come back later?"

"Carlos," said Carlos. "I don't do well with 'mister.' And I really need to have something ready by Sunday. Maybe I can help. I'm a reporter. Finding out things is what I do. Maybe we can help each other out."

"Well, maybe," said the staff member. "My name's Marissa. This is Regina. She came to our shelter eighteen months ago with a brand-new baby. Since then, she's learned English, she's studied, and she starts her new job on Monday."

Marissa looked at Regina. "She's the reason we're here. She's done everything we asked her to do to prepare for independent living. She was signing the papers today and was about to move into her own apartment over the weekend. But apparently something went wrong with the landlord. Regina, what happened?"

Regina said, "He tried to take money from my cash card, but machine said my card has no money. We call the bank and the bank tell us I bought a computer and software in San Antonio yesterday, so now my card has no money and they send me new card."

Carlos said, "I'm guessing you never went to San Antonio to buy a computer, right?"

"No!" said Regina. "Why people keep asking me this? I have no car and no driver's license. How would I get there? And what would I do with a computer?"

"I'm sorry," said Carlos. "The same thing happened to my boss today. Somebody apparently stole money from his credit card, too. I'm sure by now he's working on straightening it out. So can't you just call the bank and tell them you didn't buy that computer?"

"No," explained Marissa. "Because this isn't a credit card. It's a cash-assistance card so if anyone steals the card, whatever's on the card is gone."

"But nobody stole my card," said Regina. "Look, here it is," she said, fumbling in her purse. She found the card and showed it to Marissa and Carlos. "How can somebody steal money from my card when I have it right here? And where I live now?"

"Surely that should be easy to handle," said Carlos. "Can't you just stay in the shelter until this all gets straightened out?"

"No," said Marissa, "She can't. We can't let anyone live here more than eighteen months. It puts our funding in jeopardy."

"So when's the eighteen months up?" asked Carlos.

"Monday starts month nineteen."

"Oh, now I get it," said Carlos. "Listen, I know this looks bad. But I have an idea for a story that might help."

Marissa smiled. "Carlos, I think your timing might have been perfect."

Carlos smiled back. "Aren't you guys the people who say give it all up to God?"

"I think this will be a beautiful partnership," said Marissa.

"I not understand," said Regina. "Why you are happy?"

"Because this could work," said Carlos.

Carlos called the station to send the camera crew while Marissa found the shelter director. Carlos interviewed everyone involved—the apartment landlord even agreed to an on-camera interview to explain his side of the story. But the interview with Regina was gold. Emmy-winning stuff.

"Regina, some people will be upset that you came to the United States illegally. Why did you come here?" prompted Carlos.

"I live with my mother and brothers in Guatemala. My oldest brother, he join a gang and they help feed us. But one of my brother's friends in the gang attack me. I hurt and sick many days. But nobody believe me. Some American missionaries run a free clinic and I went there for medicine. They say I pregnant."

"That had to be a shock. What did you do?"

"My family not believe I attacked. How could my brother friend attack me when they give food to us? If they find out I pregnant, they make me leave because no money and I bring shame on family. One of the women at the clinic, she tell me she know somebody who can help and she give me money to pay. She cry. I talk to her friend and he take me to Mexico. Somebody else take me across Mexico and somebody else take me to the border at Nuevo Laredo. But the man at the border say I can't go to United States."

"How long from when you left Guatemala until you found yourself in Nuevo Laredo?" asked Carlos.

"Many months," answered Regina. "I very fat. But I pray to God every day and God tell me not to worry. I say, 'Easy for you, God, you not carrying a baby.' But God keep telling me not to worry, so I try not to worry. Two men with a van see me. They ask me if I want to come to United States and I say yes. They ask me how much money do I have and I say 2,000 pesos. So they show me how they cut out the bottom of the van and cover it up and tell me I can lie down in that space and they will take me across the border."

"For 2,000 pesos?"

"Yes. God say don't worry, so I give them the money and get in van."

"You gave them your last 2,000 pesos? How would you eat if these men stole it?"

"God told me not to worry."

"So then what happened?"

"They tell me, be very quiet. We all get in big trouble if they find me in van. I try to be quiet, but Juanita want to be born. I pray to God, 'Take me if you want—I have nothing. But let my baby live in this wonderful country.' I cry in pain while men in van talk to men in booth. Men in uniforms open the floor and ask me questions in English. But I only know how to say 'I no speak English.' So they put me in another van with lights on top. They take me to hospital and Juanita born a few minutes later. I hear everyone say this word, over and over again 'miracle.' I ask the lady who help me talk to doctors, 'What means miracle? She tell me what just happened is miracle and my baby United States citizen now. I ask what that means and she say it means nobody can make us leave. So I name my baby Juanita Miracle Lopez. Juanita after my grandmother, and Miracle because 'miracle' the first English word I learn. And Lopez after me. And I promised God I pay back everyone who helped me. And I tell God sorry for worrying."

By 5:00 p.m. Friday, Carlos had his story. On the way back to the station with the camera crew, he called Luis. "Luis, you'll love this story. I think we can have something ready for 6:00 tonight and we have material for follow-ups Saturday and Sunday."

"Good because today is a slow news day," said Luis. "Get your butt in here. You're on the air in an hour."

"I'm on the way," said Carlos. "By the way, what happened with your credit card?"

"Some kind of fraud thing apparently. They told me somebody in McAllen tried to use my credit-card number to buy a TV."

"No kidding! You and Regina have some things in common."

"Who's Regina?"

"You'll meet her in a little while on the news."

Carlos and his team worked feverishly on the story. They cut forty-five minutes of raw material down to ninety seconds and were ready by 5:59 with less than one minute to spare.

"Meet Regina Lopez and her American citizen, eighteen-month-old daughter, Juanita," said Carlos into the camera. "From a harrowing escape from poverty and crime in Guatemala to an unbelievable border crossing right here in Laredo, to an eighteen-month ordeal to educate herself and learn English, Regina proved she is a survivor." The story cut to video clips of Regina and Juanita, with sound bites from the shelter staff on Regina's remarkable journey, culminating with her new job.

"But now Regina has a problem," said Carlos's voice over video of Regina helping the shelter staff get ready for dinner. "Somebody stole all the money from her cash-assistance card and she's unable to come up with a deposit and first month's rent for an apartment. She can't stay in the shelter past eighteen months, so now her only available option is life on the streets. Streets where all doors and windows are barred," Carlos continued, as the video cut to images of the buildings with barred doors and windows.

The story cut to an interview with the shelter director, who explained, "We can't allow anyone to stay past eighteen months. If we do, we put all our funding at risk. We all knew this day was coming and we were all so happy just a few days ago because we prepared for it. Regina might be our best success story. But now this! Nobody could anticipate somebody stealing all the money from Regina's cash card. It's devastating. What kind of heartless thief steals money from the poor? And how did this happen? How did somebody get her card number?"

The next scene showed Carlos and the landlord talking, with Carlos in voiceover: "So why won't the landlord let her move in and make up the back rent later? We asked him that question and here's what he said."

"Look, I feel bad for her. But I'm not rich. I need the income from this property to pay my own bills and I have people waiting in line to sign a lease. I agreed to leave this property open for the weekend, but I can't hold it any longer. I'm sorry, but if I don't get paid, I'll end up needing one of those cash-assistance cards myself."

The story ran for ninety seconds, leaving thirty seconds for in-studio interaction.

"Carlos, that was a touching story," read the co-anchor from the teleprompter script. "What are people saying about her illegal entry?"

"Nobody's happy about that," said Carlos. He didn't need the teleprompter script. "But, at least in this one individual case, she appears determined to become an American citizen herself. She's trying to find a better life for her daughter. And after all, isn't that what our parents and grandparents did for us?"

"What does Regina do now?" the other co-anchor read from the teleprompter, using the sincere facial expressions practiced earlier with the show's producer.

"Nobody knows yet," answered Carlos, still not needing the teleprompter. "She only found out about her card this morning and apparently the government doesn't assume liability in fraud situations. So the money is gone and Regina's not sure where she'll live or what her next move might be. She can't stay in the shelter and she can't live on the streets with an eighteen-month-old baby."

"Heartbreaking," read one of the other co-anchors. "But you'll keep following the story for us, Carlos?"

"You bet," said Carlos. "The shelter's starting a fund for Regina and others in her situation, and if anyone wants to help, they can call the station to donate and we'll make sure they get it. Maybe we'll have some good news to share soon during this Christmas season."

As they went to commercial, Carlos looked at Luis watching behind the cameras and winked. Luis gave a thumbs-up signal as the muffled sound of ringing phones started echoing throughout the studio.

Jerry Barkley

Friday, December 6th was another crazy Friday for Jerry Barkley. His phone started ringing at 7:30 that morning and didn't seem to stop all day. "Why does it always ring too early the morning after a late night?" he thought to himself for about the ten-thousandth time. But that was the way his solo IT consulting business worked. Feast or famine.

By 4:00 he was done with his last meeting of the day, so barring another emergency from somebody else, his day would end early. Jerry found himself driving home, summarizing in his head the invoices he would send Monday morning and action items coming up the next week. As he drove near a Bullseye store, he remembered he needed cereal and water—breakfast in the car on the way to customers with Monday morning emergencies. As he pulled into the parking lot, he was amazed to see it so crowded. "Great," he thought. "I get to wait in line behind everyone doing their Christmas shopping so I can eat next week."

The line wasn't too bad after all. In and out in twenty minutes. He paid with his Visa credit card because the issuing bank offered a cash-back reward. As he unlocked his car, his cell phone rang. Another customer with a standard Friday afternoon emergency. A typical day in Jerry Barkley's life. The details of that Friday would blur over the next week as customer mini-crises came and went.

Monday afternoon, December 9th, the phone rang again. A sales rep with a telephone system reseller needed help with a server upgrade for one of her customers, because the server needed a new version of its operating system to work properly with the new phone system she sold them. Oh, and could he do it tomorrow morning? Because the phone system was scheduled to be installed the following afternoon, and the server needed more memory and disk space to accommodate the new system.

"Do you believe in miracles?" Jerry asked.

"I know you can work them," she said.

"Let me see what I can do."

Jerry knew the local hardware suppliers and quickly found somebody who had the necessary parts at the proper price. "Deal. Let's do this. I'll pick them up in the morning."

Jerry gave them his credit-card number and security code. And then he waited… longer than usual.

"Sorry, Jerry, it was declined."

Jerry felt that familiar tension in his gut. "I'm sure I paid that bill. What's going on? I need this like a hole in the head."

He bought the parts he needed with a different credit card, and then called the issuer, Uncle Sam Bank. After punching in his credit-card number, the last four digits of his Social Security number, and his zip code, the automated answering system at the bank said it would transfer him to the fraud department. "This might be good," he said to himself.

"I'm sorry, I do not understand that request. Do you want to speak to a representative?"

"Aw, nuts. Yes. *Representative*," he yelled.

"Please speak or use your telephone keypad to enter your sixteen-digit credit-card number."

"Are we going through this again?"

"I'm sorry, I do not understand that request. Transferring to an operator."

This time, Jerry remained silent. Somebody answered after six rings.

"Hi, my name's April, how may I help you?"

"Hi, April, you sound like you live in the United States!"

"Well, last time I checked, Rapid City, South Dakota, was still in this country. Can I get your name, your account number, and last four digits of your Social?"

Jerry gave her what she needed, and his billing zip code when she asked.

"Great, thanks. Now, how may I help you?"

"I just tried to buy some stuff with this credit card and it was declined. Did I forget to pay you?"

"Let me take a look. Oh—I see this was marked with a fraud tag. Let me get you right over to that department."

"Wait a minute! A fraud tag—what does that mean?"

"I really don't know, only that the fraud department would like to speak to you."

"Hey, I know someone in that department. I don't remember her name—uhh, do you have a Ms. Blue Jeans there?"

"Sir, this is Rapid City. We all wear blue jeans. Please hold."

"I'd better find that business card she gave me—the Bullseye card."

Jerry waited on hold and eight rings before somebody answered.

"Hello, Jerry, this is June with the fraud department. How may we help you?"

"Hi, June. Why are you declining my card?"

"Um, Jerry, did you do any traveling over the past weekend?"

"No, unless you count the trip to St. Paul to pick up some receptacles."

"Did you buy anything in Duluth, Minnesota or Madison, Wisconsin?"

"Not that I know of. But I buy lots of stuff online, maybe some of that could have come from there. But it isn't likely."

"We show an eighty-inch wide-screen TV bought in Duluth and a gaming system in Madison. Both purchases were on Saturday about a half hour apart. And they total more than $10,000. Those transactions triggered a fraud alert. We declined them and froze the credit card."

"Oh wow, you guys saved my rear end—thanks!"

"You're welcome. So those weren't your purchases?"

"No. No way! Why would I go to Duluth to buy a TV when I could buy one right here?"

"Our fraud-alert system probably asked the same question."

"Well, June, thanks. Hey—ya know what, I do computer security for a living. I know this is a hassle and you have to send me a new credit card, but maybe we can do something to catch these clowns."

"What did you have in mind?"

"Do you have a way to flag this number so if anyone uses it again, they'll know to call the police?"

"No. And even if we could, it probably doesn't do any good. Once a thief gets a decline on a stolen card, they get rid of it and get a new one."

"Yeah, that makes sense. Can we call the merchants and find out details on the transactions? Maybe law enforcement can track them down if we get them some data."

"Most people don't want to bother."

"I'm not most people. I do security for a living and it would make me feel good to nail one of these clowns."

"We can try if you want, but law enforcement typically doesn't do much."

"Well, let's at least try."

After an hour on the phone, June and Jerry tracked down both merchants and even talked to the store clerks at both stores who handled the transactions. A caller tried to place both orders over the phone and wanted the items shipped to a post-office box in Minneapolis. June and Jerry gathered dates and times, descriptions, transaction IDs, and the exact items the credit-card thief tried to buy.

"June, thank you for your help. I owe you a monster debt. Tell the fraud guys their systems are great. When I call the FBI and report all this, how do they get in touch with you?"

"They can call the toll-free number and ask for the fraud department. There's no direct line to me."

"Ya know… I met a lady who went to work in your department back around March or so. She likes blue jeans. She probably works in the same skyway as the Minneapolis FBI office. If I can find her phone number, why don't I send the FBI to her?"

"Probably best to just give them our toll-free number."

"What are my odds?"

"Not good. They don't follow up with this kind of stuff. Too small for them to chase and too much work."

"Ten-thousand dollars is too small?"

"For them, yeah. If you were a big corporation, they might pay attention. Or if somebody stole millions of dollars from you. But this, no, they won't care."

"Well, I gotta try. If we don't go after this, what's to stop them next time? Maybe the next fraud department won't be as good as yours."

"Good luck."

"Thanks. You've probably heard all this before."

"Something like that."

"Well, thanks for your help. If I get anywhere, I'll call the fraud department back and ask them to track you down and I'll give you an update."

"I'd like that."

Jerry's next call went to the Minneapolis FBI office. He had dealt with the FBI before—there was the embezzlement case in the late '90s that took five, count 'em, five years to resolve. And a security breach in one of Jerry's own systems in late 2000 that they wouldn't look at. He still had a hard time believing he'd had to explain what the Internet was to the lady who answered the phone, and that she didn't believe him.

But this was thirteen years later, and by now everyone would know what the Internet was, right? Even if the FBI was less than impressive in the past, this was the law enforcement agency for reporting this stuff. Jerry knew the name of a contact in the office this time, so he would ask for Agent Connor Duncan to get past the receptionist.

The tactic worked and a few seconds later, he was connected.

"Hey, Agent Duncan, my name's Jerry Barkley. We met at an InfraGard meeting a couple years ago and worked on a virus infection with a customer who didn't want to report it."

"Okay."

"This time I have a credit-card fraud and a victim eager to cooperate."

"Okay, so what have you got for me?"

"I have names, dates, transaction IDs, and a description of the thief. And I'm the victim."

"Great. Put it all in an email and send it over."

"I'm way ahead of you. I have it all ready to go. What's your email address?"

Agent Duncan gave Jerry his email address and Jerry sent it off. "It should hit your inbox any second."

"Yeah, it just came in. Okay, so some of this happened in Duluth and some in Madison?"

"Apparently."

"How much did you lose?"

"I didn't lose anything. The bank fraud group caught it."

"Uh-huh."

"What does 'uh-huh' mean?"

"It means we won't put any effort into this."

"Whaddya mean? Somebody stole my credit-card number and tried to steal more than $10,000 with it. This clown is out there doing it to somebody else right now while we're talking."

"I'll forward this to Duluth and Madison and maybe somebody will get back to you."

"So that's it? Somebody tries to steal more than $10,000; I track down all the details; I do all the legwork; and you guys don't lift a finger?"

"The honest answer, Jerry: you're too small and we don't care about you."

"And that's why fraud runs rampant. Maybe I'm in the wrong business. I should start stealing for a living."

"If you start stealing for a living, we'll come find you."

"Thanks a bunch, Connor."

"Listen, I'll forward this and if anything turns up, they'll get in touch with you. But don't hold your breath."

"You're full of good news today."

"Yeah, I know. But do you know how many leads like this come in every single day?"

"No, Connor, I don't. How many leads do you get where a victim hands you transaction details with dates, IDs, descriptions, and a bank-fraud department willing to track it down?"

"Okay, not many with that much detail. And that's the only reason I'm forwarding this one, because you gave me details that may be usable. But the unfortunate truth is, we don't have the manpower to follow up on all these cases and we probably won't follow up with this one."

"So, what, we're all on our own with stuff like this?"

"I wouldn't characterize it that way, no."

"Well if the United States Federal Bureau of Investigation doesn't want to bother investigating this stuff, who will?"

"You can work with your issuing bank-fraud department."

"I did that. And I brought it to you. And you're blowing me off."

"Your bank assumes any liability from credit-card fraud, so there isn't much we can do for you."

"What happens if I find this guy myself and I shoot him?"

"Then we'll probably come after you."

***

Jerry turned his home office upside-down the rest of Monday. He finally found what he was looking for after midnight: a Bullseye business card with the office number scratched out and the cell number circled.

"Oh yeah, that's her name, Jesse Jonsen. How could I have forgotten?"

He had trouble sleeping that night. "How do I teach these clowns they picked on the wrong victim?"

At 8:15 Tuesday morning, on the way to his emergency server upgrade project and between bites of cereal, he dialed his cell phone. After a few rings he heard, "Uncle Sam Bank, this is Jesse."

"Hey, is this the lady with the nice blue jeans?"

"What the—oh, is this you, Jerry Barkley?"

"Groovy! You remembered my name!"

"I happen to be holding your business card in my hand. I just had a long talk with June in our department about you."

"Huh! Whaddya know! I hope I wasn't too hard on her."

"No, not at all. You impressed her. She said she likes the way you think. We were in a training class last month and after you mentioned the lady with the blue jeans in Minneapolis, she called me. Her call center's getting buried and she figured I might want some help tracking down why. So I'm glad you called. I might have some work for you."

"If it has anything to do with those crooks ripping me off, I'm interested."

"It does. When can you come in to talk about it?"

"I'm on my way to a server upgrade halfway to St. Cloud. Should be done early afternoon and I'll call you on the way back."

"Sounds good. I'll see you this afternoon."

Getting Organized

"Agent Duncan, you're the point man on this one," said Edward Lang, head of the FBI Cybercrimes Task Force in Quantico, Virginia. "So far, seven banks across the country are reporting massive card fraud, and the only commonality we can see is Bullseye Stores. That puts you at ground zero. Their headquarters is six blocks from your office. What a lucky coincidence."

As the agent in charge of investigating white-collar crimes in the upper Midwest, Connor Duncan specialized in financial crimes and cybercrimes. He cut his teeth on the Sears/TRW data breach in the '80s, and had been the national go-to guy on such crimes ever since. His next assignment was right under his nose in downtown Minneapolis.

"And I'm sure I don't need to remind you, Agent Duncan, that Kenneth Moline chairs the Senate Intelligence Committee, and our budget's up for review."

Senator Moline's grandfather founded Bullseye, and Kenneth used his inherited wealth to become one of the most powerful men on Capitol Hill.

"So don't charge in like a cowboy like you usually do. Try not to step on any toes, Duncan. Play it cordial this time, you got that?"

"Okay," said Agent Duncan. "Yes, I understand. I'll try the quiet approach first. I've got my book on etiquette right here. I'll give it a speed read."

"Cut the crap, Duncan. And don't try to go grandstanding either."

"Yes, sir."

He hung up his phone and sat up in his chair. That familiar adrenaline rush was coming on. "This should be fun."

Pushing fifty, he still had a full head of bushy gray hair and a paunch from too much fast food after screwing up two marriages. He knew he would never be promoted in the bureau. He acted too independently for the bureau's taste. But he lived for assignments like this and the supervisors knew he got results, so they put up with each other.

He needed to get busy. The problem was getting worse every minute. He turned to his computer, found the Bullseye website, and looked at "Meet The Management Team." Daniel Berger was CEO. Liz Isaacs was CIO. One of them would be the logical person to call. He found a phone number on the website and dialed it.

"Hello, and welcome to Bullseye Stores!" said an enthusiastic recorded voice on the phone. "Press 1 to find a store near you. Press 2 to inquire about an online order. Press 3 for our gift registry. Press 4 for promotions, sweepstakes, and discounts. Press 5 for product and safety recalls. Press 6 for media relations. Press 7 for job inquiries. Or press 9 to speak to a team member who will be happy to assist you!"

Connor pressed 9. "Due to a heavier than normal call volume, we are experiencing longer than usual wait times. Please wait for the next available agent, who will be happy to assist you!"

But the wait was less than five minutes and he soon found himself talking to a pleasant voice with a slight Scandinavian accent. "Hello, this is Evelyn and how may I help you today?"

"Hi. This is Special Agent Connor Duncan with the FBI in Minneapolis and I need to speak to Daniel Berger right now, please."

Evelyn seemed ready for this. "Mr. Berger's unavailable at the moment. Is there something I can do to help you?"

"Probably not. Somebody's using your store to steal credit cards on a massive scale. I need to talk to your CEO right now about that."

"Sir, before we go any further, please know that this call is being recorded and we prosecute prank calls." Connor detected an edge to Evelyn's voice. This was to be expected—this was not a run of the mill customer call.

"Evelyn, I need you to put away your flowchart and connect me to a manager. Right now. I won't ask again."

"Please hold."

After a few minutes, a manager named Glen came on the line. "Um, Special Agent Duncan is it? How may I help you? And do you know how many calls we get every day that say they're with the FBI?"

"I don't care how many calls you get. As I just told Evelyn, somebody's using your store to steal credit cards on a massive scale. I need to talk to your boss's boss's boss right now."

"I'm sorry, sir, but we can't do that."

"You can't or you won't?"

"We don't have a direct line with Mr. Berger's office."

"He has a phone, doesn't he?"

"I'm sure he does, but we can't send callers right to him. That's why Bullseye operates this call center."

"Okay, fine. I just told you somebody's using your store to steal credit-card numbers on a massive scale. Now what are you going to do about it? I suggest you shut down all your credit-card operations right now."

There was silence on the phone for about five seconds.

"Um, sir, I don't know who you are, but this is not funny."

"No, it definitely is not funny. I told you who I am and I told you what needs to happen. If you can't call your CEO, maybe there's a manager above you who can."

"Our call center is in North Dakota. That's why we don't know how to call Mr. Berger."

"Uff-da!" said Connor, and he promptly hung up. "What a waste of time. I'll call their PR person. At least they'll be at corporate headquarters and not out in the middle of nowhere. Here it is, Brittany Chatsworth."

He dialed and someone picked up on the third ring. "That's more like it."

"Brittany Chatsworth, Corporate Communications. How may I help you?"

"I'm Special Agent Connor Duncan. I'm with the Minneapolis FBI office and I specialize in financial crime. I need to talk to your boss right now, because we have reason to believe your company's in the middle of an international credit-card racket. Every time one of your customers swipes a credit card, the number goes over to Russia and pops up again locally in the form of bogus plastic."

"Oh, my."

"Yep, oh my. I have messages from seven major banks so far today. They've all found new batches of credit cards up for sale from somebody in Russia. All those credit cards have only one thing in common—they were all used at your store. Recently. Like after Black Friday."

"My gosh."

"And by golly! So what are we going to do about this, Ms. Chatsworth?"

"Agent Duncan, I'm sure we're not a party to some fraud ring, and I know our computer security is the finest in the world."

"I'm sure it is, Ms. Chatsworth, but if I don't get through to a decision-maker quickly, I have an emergency warrant in my hand to shut you down. All it needs is a signature from any pissed-off federal judge who shopped at your store last week. Give me your fax number and I'll send you a copy."

Getting Organized

"Agent Duncan!"

"Let's start over. Ms. Chatsworth, ma'am, I need to speak with Mr. Daniel Berger please. It's urgent."

"I'm sorry, but he truly is unavailable. He's out of the country at some very important meetings."

"And I'm sure he's enjoying himself. In that case, may I please speak to the person in charge of all your technology? Please? Ma'am?"

"Why certainly, that's an excellent idea. That would be Liz Isaacs. She's our CIO. She gets out of her executive council meeting in a little over an hour."

"Ms. Chatsworth, I'm only a fifteen-minute walk from your lobby. But I have a message from my boss in Quantico about Federal Judge Marvin Thornton, right here in Minneapolis. Apparently he has a problem with a credit card. As long as I'm waiting, should I stop at the Federal Building on the way to your lobby and tell him where his problem started?"

"Agent Duncan!"

"While we were talking, the Russians stole about a thousand more card numbers from your customers. What's it gonna be?"

"Very well, Agent Duncan. I'll meet you in the lobby in fifteen minutes with Ms. Isaacs."

"Thank you, ma'am. I look forward to meeting you."

"The pleasure will be all mine."

After a brisk walk through the Minneapolis skyways, Agent Duncan, armed with summaries of reports from the banks that had called so far, found a concerned-looking woman with graying hair wrapped into a bun at the main receptionist desk, along with another, taller brunette woman who looked like somebody in charge.

"Agent Duncan, I presume?" said Brittany.

"That's right," said Agent Duncan, showing his badge. "Ms. Chatsworth and Ms. Isaacs?"

"Yes, I'm Brittany Chatsworth and this is Liz Isaacs, our CIO. I pulled Liz out of an executive briefing to come meet you on your urgent business."

"Nice to meet you both," said Agent Duncan. "Can we sit down in a conference room for a minute?"

A few minutes later, Agent Duncan laid out what he had so far. "And this is what we have from Uncle Sam Bank. They're right down the street and I can get them over here in a few minutes if you want. They think by now they have five or six million of their cards up for sale on this website. Add up what all the other banks found and we're at around thirty million cards. And counting. And the one thing all the samples the banks bought back have in common—they were all used at a Bullseye sometime after Black Friday. You guys have a problem. A big one."

"Wait a minute," said Liz. "That doesn't prove anything. Nearly everyone in the country will buy something in one of our stores, and most of them use credit cards. It only makes sense they'd all have us in common. And do you know what shutting down our credit-card operations would do to our holiday sales figures?"

"Not my concern," said Agent Duncan. "You want proof? Uncle Sam Bank started a test last Friday. They issued ten special cards to key employees across the country. Each of them went to a different Bullseye and bought one item, then reported the transaction back to their fraud department. After the test buys, the fraud department set up alerts for those ten credit cards. If anyone anywhere tries to use those numbers again, their fraud department will know about it immediately and they'll tell us. Those cards were only used at one of your stores, one time. That's it. So if anyone, anywhere else tries to use those cards, we'll know the numbers came from here. That will be your proof."

Brittany looked at Liz. Liz fidgeted slightly in her seat, trying to remain composed.

Agent Duncan continued. "If you make us wait until that proof is in and a few million more people have their credit-card numbers stolen, we will shut you down."

More silence.

"Can they do that?" asked Brittany.

"No," said Liz, now looking square at Agent Duncan. "No, they can't."

Agent Duncan met Liz's gaze. "You don't want to test us," he said. "We can and we will. We have the home phone numbers of every federal judge in the United States and my boss is on the phone with one of them right now."

He paused to let this all sink in and then continued in a softer tone.

"I have about thirty million fraud victims—and climbing—and they all came from here. I've given you enough evidence already and you know it. Now, just because we can shut you down doesn't mean we want to shut you down. What we want is for you to find and fix this mess before it gets any worse. So my boss asked me to give you some time to react. Find your leak and plug it. We'll even help track down the source. Let's do this the easy way. Everyone loses if we do it the hard way."

Agent Duncan sat back in his chair and looked Liz in the eye.

"Do we have a deal?"

Liz was careful. After a long pause, she said, "Of course, it would take the CEO or possibly the board of directors to freeze our entire operation. However, I do have the authority to agree to a joint review of our system, but I would insist that our server operations director be a part of the investigation. He'll show you we haven't done anything wrong and our system is secure."

Agent Duncan leaned forward in his chair. "On behalf of the United States Federal Bureau of Investigation, thank you for your eagerness to cooperate. Uncle Sam Bank also wants to help find out what's going on."

"Why not just put the whole thing on Facebook and get everyone involved?" smirked Liz.

"Now, now, Ms. Isaacs. I do believe you're being facetious. Our joint forensics team will be here this afternoon. I'll send you the details soon. Thank you both."

After Agent Duncan left, Liz got on her phone and said, "Get Ryan MacMillan to my office right away… What?… I don't care if he's sick. Get his fanny downtown now. I don't give a flying leap what he has! You tell him that."

***

By 1:00 p.m. Jerry was back in his car, inbound on I-94 to downtown Minneapolis. "Hey, Jesse, I'm on my way in."

"Good. How far away are you?"

"Not quite an hour away. I need a favor."

"Oh no, here come the outrageous demands…"

"I need a place where I can park for free."

"That's pretty outrageous all right, but I'll make it happen."

"One more thing."

"Are you one of those guy divas or what?"

"I'm wearing my tennis shoes. Anyone at your downtown bank have a problem with that?"

"I'm still wearing blue jeans."

"Groovy. See you this afternoon."

"Did you really just say 'groovy'?"

"Yup."

***

Jerry rode the elevator up from the parking garage and made his way to the main lobby at Uncle Sam Bank, where Jesse met him.

"You made it here five minutes early," said Jesse. "Nice tennis shoes." She reached to shake Jerry's hand.

Jerry shook her hand. "Nice blue jeans."

They both laughed, just like old times.

"Nice to see you, Jesse. I gotta tell you I was a little nervous leaving my car in the reserved area," said Jerry, "but they checked my license plates and said I was fine."

"I try to keep my word," said Jesse. "We don't have much time. Let's go down to my office for a few minutes and I'll fill you in."

"Down? They didn't give you a corner office on the top floor?"

"Well I am in the corner, but there's not much of a view, I'm afraid. No windows. And we're meeting with the FBI in a few minutes."

"Really? They blew me off when *I* called."

***

A half hour into his briefing, the room got so warm that Jerry took off his sweater.

"I wish you did have a window so we could open it. Didn't they give you any air conditioning either?"

"Sorry about that. The heat from all the computer equipment down here pretty much overwhelms the AC." Looking at the clock, Jesse continued, "I've shared everything I've got with you. Any questions?"

"Just one. Why call me in on this? You must have a dozen IT security experts at your disposal right here at corporate."

"Well, yeah, I could probably get their help. But they're too… *corporate*. I need creativity. And it takes time and paperwork to get them. I don't have time and I hate paperwork. And now it turns out you're also a victim. I figure that probably gives you a pretty strong motivation to go after these guys."

"You got that right."

"So that's why you're here. C'mon, we gotta go."

***

Jesse and Jerry met Agent Duncan in the skyway bank lobby. "Agent Duncan, this is Jerry Barkley," said Jesse. "I hired him as a special consultant to help track down the problem."

Agent Duncan gave Jerry a once-over as they shook hands. His sweeping glance ended at Jerry's shoes. "Pleased to meet you, Jerry. Now why does your name sound familiar?"

"Probably from when you blew me off when I called you last week."

"Oh, that guy. Heh heh. So, you think you know a lot about IT security, do ya?"

"I do IT security work," said Jerry. "I build firewalls, manage a bunch of servers, and I do soup-to-nuts IT support." Jerry couldn't help himself. "And I learned last week that law enforcement won't help victims, so I think I'll write a book."

"I probably had that coming. Whose firewalls do you sell?"

"My own. I build them using a bunch of open-source software tools."

"Why?"

"Because if I'm managing a network, I need a tool at the boundary I can count on and none of the commercial stuff I looked at gives me what I need. And I'm pigheaded enough to believe I can do it better than they can."

"Have you found success with that?"

"It keeps me in good tennis shoes."

Getting Organized

"I can see that."

"So you're not a bank employee?" asked Agent Duncan.

"No, I'm not. I'm a customer though."

"What's your company name?"

"Barkley IT Services," said Jerry.

"I see," said Agent Duncan. "So why are you here right now?"

"Because my friend, Jesse, asked me to be here," said Jerry. "Plus, I want to help nail the clowns who stole my credit card. With or without your help."

"We have all the skill sets we need inside the FBI," said Agent Duncan.

"Maybe," said Jerry. "I'm sure when you fill out all the proper forms in triplicate and get approval from seven layers of bureaucrats in Washington, you can get somebody here next month. But I'm here right now."

Agent Duncan looked at Jerry and paused. Jesse started to say something but Agent Duncan stopped her. Then he smiled. "First of all, we haven't filled out forms in triplicate since before Reagan was president. And second, I don't care what contractors you bring in, and you'd be surprised at what we can do fast when we need it. And third, welcome to the team."

"How big is this team going to be?"

"Well, I'm on orders from my top boss to be magnanimous on this case, so I've agreed to work with both the bank and Bullseye on forming a mini-forensics team for our first sweep. In fact I'm waiting for their server guy, Ryan MacMillan. He's running late."

***

Ryan was an hour late. He showed up wearing an oversized trench coat and a long scarf. As he stepped inside the conference room, he let out a huge, uncovered sneeze. Everybody cringed.

"This better be important," proclaimed Ryan. "I'm sick, you know."

Jesse deftly handed Ryan a box of tissues. After he thoroughly wiped his nose and stuffed the used tissue up his sleeve, he looked up with his watery eyes and surveyed the crowd.

"Jesse, so this is where you went after Bullseye! Too bad they have you locked up in this overheated dungeon." And turning his gaze to Jerry, he said, "I know you. You're the guy with the tennis shoes and the sweater. Where's the sweater?"

"It got hot."

"Ryan," interrupted Jesse, "this is Jerry Barkley, he's working on special assignment for our bank. And over here we have Agent Connor Duncan from the FBI."

Ryan's condescending smile slipped to a frown when he looked at Agent Duncan.

"Oh, so you're the reason I had to come to work. Now I'll know where to send my medical bills when I get pneumonia."

Everyone waved politely to Ryan, in lieu of shaking hands. Jesse proceeded to lay out all the banking information, and Agent Duncan summarized what he had heard from the other banks across the country.

When he wasn't sneezing, Ryan spent most of the briefing staring up at the ceiling or checking his cell phone.

When dinnertime came, Jesse had a couple of pizzas sent in. Ryan picked through all of them.

"Did you have to get mushrooms on every piece? I hate mushrooms, ya know."

The other three decided they weren't hungry.

For the next few hours Ryan explained over and over exactly how such a break-in was inconceivable. The other three peppered him with questions, which he either ignored or gave the same pat answers. He'd wrap up by saying, "You guys just don't understand our system.

Let me explain it again…"

It was around midnight when he was about to launch his fiftieth variation on that theme.

"Wait a minute," said Jerry, "We're missing something here. Those credit-card dumps had zip codes, right?"

"So what?" said Ryan. "You're not listening to me."

"Yeah," said Jesse. "Every one of them had a zip code. That's why they're premium priced. You're more likely to get away with a fake card if you use it in the same zip code."

"So, how'd they get zip codes?" asked Jerry. "Those guys knew the store zip code for every credit card. Why are we holed up in a conference room? We need to look at a store."

"What?"

"We need to go to a store and follow a transaction."

"Wait a minute," said Ryan. "The only place I'm going when I leave here is to my warm bed at home. You want us to drive over to a store and have a field trip? Forget it."

"No," interrupted Agent Duncan. "It's a good idea. Let's follow a transaction."

"Yeah, exactly," said Jerry. "Let's go shopping. I've got Wireshark ready to go on my laptop."

"Wireshark?" asked Ryan.

Jerry and Agent Duncan looked at each other. Jerry rolled his eyes. Agent Duncan stifled a grin. "It's an open-source network monitoring tool," said Agent Duncan.

"Ryan," said Agent Duncan, in the gruffer range of his voice. "If you ever want to see your bed again, get us into a store right away."

"Jesse," said Jerry, "get some sleep."

"Thanks," said Jesse. "Guys, I don't speak geek, but I have an idea. While you're doing your thing, think about how we can make some lemonade."

Jerry smiled. "I'll email you with what we find."

Agent Duncan looked at Jerry. "It's a long story," said Jerry.

***

Lake Street store manager Greta Olavsen smiled as she pulled the hot-buttered rum out of the microwave. Greta was a big, broad, blonde Swede who had worked her way up from cashier to manager. After a long day at work during the height of the Christmas sales season, and with the kids finally asleep, it was time for Greta and her husband to put their feet up and watch a movie.

Her cell phone rang around 12:30 a.m. Greta answered on the fifth ring.

"Um, Greta, this is Ryan MacMillan with the IT department. I understand you're the manager of the Lake Street store?"

"That's right. It's not on fire or anything?"

"No, no. It's really nothing," said Ryan. "But I have an FBI agent and another guy, and they say we need you to open your store so they can do some tests."

Greta stifled a yawn. "Is this like a fire drill?"

"I wish it was."

Thirty minutes later, Greta, Agent Duncan, Jerry, and Ryan met in the Lake Street store parking lot. Greta unlocked the door and everyone walked inside.

Ryan introduced everyone. Agent Duncan took over.

"Greta, we're sorry to inconvenience you, but we're investigating a possible data breach at Bullseye. Someone's stealing millions of credit-card numbers, and we think we can find the leak if we tap into a transaction. We need you to open a point-of-sale terminal."

"You mean a checkout counter?"

"Exactly. Now who wants to buy something?"

"I could really use some cold medicine," said Ryan. "But I think I'll just pay cash."

"What's the matter, Ryan," chided Jerry. "Afraid to use your ATM card?"

"No, it's not that," bluffed Ryan. "It's just that I get 20 percent off and the whole thing gets complicated. Plus, I don't want you guys looking at my number."

"Yeah, right," said Jerry. "I think I'll get a couple of sandwiches from the deli counter. You guys want some cereal? I'm starved."

"Get a couple for me, too," said Agent Duncan. "Suddenly my appetite came back."

"Okay," said Jerry, "but first let me set up my packet sniffer." Jerry disconnected the network cable from the back of a cash register and connected the cable to his laptop. Then he connected a crossover cable from the other network adapter in his laptop to the POS subsystem.

"What is all that?" asked Greta.

"It's kind of like wiretapping a phone call," said Jerry. "When we buy the sandwiches, we'll capture the whole transaction. Then we'll dig into it and see what we find. Okay, fire it up."

While Jerry and Agent Duncan wandered over to the deli section, Greta turned on the POS terminal in front of the laptop.

They ran the transaction and Jerry swiped his card. "Okay, let's see what we've got. You can see, I recorded every conversation your POS terminal had with everyone else when I paid for these sandwiches with my credit card. Your POS terminal had to ask somebody if my credit card was okay, and then it had to process the transaction. That's what all these numbers and letters on my laptop mean."

Jerry and Agent Duncan spent the next thirty minutes eating their sandwiches and looking at rows of unintelligible letters and numbers. Greta watched patiently while Ryan wiped his nose and looked bored.

"So what's the verdict?" asked Greta.

"Nothing jumps out," said Jerry. "But we're not done looking yet. This isn't like the movies where some computer whiz types three characters and saves the world. It's a lot more tedious in real life."

"Do you have a copy of Process Explorer handy?" asked Agent Duncan.

"Good idea," said Jerry.

"What's Process Explorer?" asked Greta.

"It's a diagnostic tool that might be helpful. Your POS terminal is really an old Windows computer and we can use the same diagnostic tools on it we use on other Windows systems," explained Agent Duncan.

"I have a copy on this USB memory stick," said Jerry. "You okay if I load it?"

"If you must," said Ryan. "But if you crash our system, you'll pay for it. I helped design it you know."

"Yeah. Where have I heard that?" muttered Jerry.

"What have we here?" asked Agent Duncan, looking at the Process Explorer summary display. "Hey Mr. Designer, what's this process named GreenPOS?"

"I don't know," said Ryan, becoming more annoyed. "Probably something the app team added. I wouldn't worry about it if I were you."

"I wonder what it has open," said Jerry as he clicked through Process Explorer screens. "What's in C:\System32\Twain_32\zhcfghilkc\McTrayErrorLogging.dll? Hey Connor, does this look suspicious to you?"

"Hmmm," said Ryan, now becoming a little curious.

"Huh?" asked Greta.

"It's sitting in a subdirectory with a random name underneath 'Twain underscore 32.' But that directory is used mostly for scanner drivers," said Jerry. "Why is this DLL file sitting there?"

"That doesn't make sense," said Agent Duncan.

"Unless it's not really a DLL, just named that way to hide," said Jerry. "What if somebody disguised some data to make it look like a program?"

"You are one paranoid cowboy," said Ryan. "So do you spray door-knobs with disinfectant before you grab 'em?"

Agent Duncan said, "We've seen this before. If you want to hide from guys like me, this is a decent way to do it. But before we get done here, we're going to sniff this guy out like a bloodhound after a rabbit."

"Works for me," said Jerry as he finished the last bites of his sandwich and a handful of cereal. He launched Notepad and opened that DLL file. "Well, whaddya know about that?"

"Holy moly!" said Agent Duncan.

"*What*?!" asked Greta.

"It's a copy of my name and credit-card number," said Jerry. "And names and credit-card numbers for about fifteen other customers." Pointing to the screen he asked, "Hey Greta, what's the zip code here?"

"Oh my goodness sakes!" said Greta, as she looked at the screen.

"That's your zip code, right?" asked Jerry.

"Yes. On every single line."

"This stuff is supposed to be encrypted," said Agent Duncan.

"Yup," said Jerry.

"So how come it's not?" asked Greta.

"Ryan, you might want to ask your app developers that question. I have a hunch they'll tell you this isn't their file. They didn't do this."

"So who did?" asked Greta.

"Whoever's stealing credit-card numbers from everyone who shops here," said Jerry.

"Oh, baloney," said Ryan. "It's just an encryption issue. I'll write up a change request on it for the app team."

"I'm telling you, your POS terminals are infected with malware and they're stealing credit-card numbers from your customers," said Jerry.

"Malware—that's like a virus, right?" asked Greta.

"Yup," said Jerry. "Somebody planted that malware in here. And now there are millions of card numbers up for sale on an underground Russian website. And this GreenPOS program helped send them over there. Every time anyone buys anything from your store, somebody in Russia is robbing them."

"How do you know?" asked Greta.

Before Jerry could answer, Agent Duncan explained, "Look at what we uncovered. Somebody's disguising these data files as part of a program and burying them in directories where nobody would normally look."

"Wait a minute," said Ryan. "We have a firewall and antivirus software all over the place. Our security is stronger than Fort Knox. There's absolutely no way a malevolent program could get in here."

"And yet here it is," said Jerry. "Virus scanners only work with known signatures. I'll bet none of the virus scanners have seen this one yet and they won't find it."

"Let's try another program—let's see what Autoruns tells us," said Jerry.

A few minutes later, Agent Duncan and Jerry stared at the Autoruns display.

"There it is," said Agent Duncan.

"Yup. Starts as a service," said Jerry.

Ryan stayed silent this time, wiping his nose as Jerry and Agent Duncan worked.

Jerry clicked "Start"… "Control Panel"… "Administrative Tools"… "Services," and scrolled down a few lines.

"You guys have a clean POS terminal back at corporate, right?" asked Jerry, looking at Ryan.

"Duh," said Ryan.

"There it is," said Jerry, pointing to a window on the screen. "You won't have autoruns, so here's what it looks like from the 'services' applet. But you won't see this on your clean one. This is your culprit."

"So where did you come from?" asked Jerry, deep in thought. "Can we grab a couple of chairs?"

"Why don't we just take this terminal back to my office," suggested Greta. "We can plug it in back there."

Jerry looked at Greta, then at Agent Duncan. "Wait a minute—Ryan, are all these POS terminals on the same Ethernet segment as everything else in the store?"

"Yeah, what about it?" asked Ryan.

"So what regulates who these POS terminals can talk to?" asked Jerry.

"Software on the POS terminals," said Ryan. "They talk to credit-card processors and the store domain controller and database server. That's it."

"But what if that software gets messed up," countered Jerry, "or somebody loads bad software onto those things? Nobody will stop them from talking with anyone they want."

"That can't happen," said Ryan. "It's all internal."

"Really! So how do you explain what we just found?" asked Jerry. "Put a firewall in front of these things. That gives you an extra layer of defense."

"What are you guys talking about?" asked Greta.

Agent Duncan explained, "You may have a wall surrounding your city but you also need another wall surrounding your crown jewels in case somebody breaches the city wall."

Greta nodded. Ryan stared straight ahead, dumbstruck.

"That gives me an idea," said Jerry. "I want to capture all the traffic in and out of this POS terminal when we boot it."

"Yeah. Good call," said Agent Duncan, nodding.

"I don't get it," said Greta.

"Just a hunch," said Jerry. "Somebody loaded that software onto that terminal and set it up to run as a service, right? Our Russian friends didn't do it by hand. You have, what, fifteen POS terminals in this store? And more than 2,000 stores around the country? That adds up to a lot of POS terminals. Somebody had to set up some automation to load that program on all your POS terminals across the country. The natural time to load it is when they boot. If we watch this one boot, maybe we can find its mother ship. I still have everything connected, so let's just boot it here. I'll capture the data packets and then we'll go back to Greta's office and look them over."

Greta shut down the POS terminal as Jerry clicked buttons on his laptop to save the original Wireshark packet capture and start a new one.

"Ready?" asked Greta.

"Fire it up," said Jerry.

Twenty minutes later, all four sat in Greta's office, huddled around Jerry's laptop.

"I can filter all the stuff to and from known IP addresses we don't care about," said Jerry. "That leaves these few to look at."

After clicking on a few packets, Jerry asked, "What's at IP address 10.2.128.20 named 'update44128'?"

"That must be one of the update servers at corporate," said Ryan. "No reason to be alarmed."

"So why is a POS terminal doing NetBIOS with a server at corporate?" asked Jerry.

"Hmmph," said Ryan, his patience growing thin. "Haven't you ever heard of Windows Update?"

"On a POS terminal? At boot time? Not buyin' it," said Agent Duncan.

"What's NetBIOS?" asked Greta.

"NetBIOS is the way Microsoft reads and writes files on another computer. When this POS terminal boots, it's reading something from the server at 10.2.128.20 named 'update44128.' That seems fishy to me. Why is a POS terminal reading something from a server at corporate when it boots?"

"Good question," said Jerry. "Let's find out." Jerry clicked some buttons to expand the data portion of this packet. "Well, will you look at that."

Agent Duncan took a close look. "I don't believe it."

"Don't believe what?" asked Greta.

"It's grabbing a copy of that program that reads credit-card numbers—GreenPOS—from that server at corporate," said Agent Duncan. "Somebody compromised that server!"

"Yup," said Jerry. "And if those POS terminals in the stores were walled off with even some basic auditing at the boundary, you could have stopped this attack before it ever started."

"Idle speculation," said Ryan.

Jerry thought for a few seconds. "Let's try the next step. Greta, can we use your computer?"

"Sure," said Greta. "What are you thinking?"

"I want to log on to that server as the administrator and see what we find," said Jerry. "And I want to look at the GPOs on your domain controller."

"What's a GPO?" asked Greta.

"Group Policy Object," said Agent Duncan. "Jerry wants to find out what marching orders these things get when they boot."

"Let's say you're a Russian thief," said Jerry, "and you want 20,000 or more systems to run your evil program. How would you load that program onto all those systems? Even if it takes only two minutes per system to do it by hand, that's 40,000 minutes, or almost 700 hours of labor."

"Okay," said Greta.

"So instead of loading it by hand 20,000 times, what if you could set up some automation so all those POS terminals would load it the next time they boot?" asked Jerry.

"Yeah, I'd probably do it that way," said Greta.

"But before we go GPO hunting on your domain controller," said Jerry, "let's go GreenPOS hunting. Ryan, what's your administrator password?"

"I'm not giving that to you guys," said Ryan.

"Okay, fine," said Agent Duncan. "Hop on Greta's computer and start up two RDP sessions for us. One to this store's domain controller and one to that update server at corporate."

Ten minutes later, Jerry was at the keyboard with Agent Duncan and Greta looking on.

"Hey, Connor—where did my packet capture say GreenPOS lives?" asked Jerry.

"D Temp, and dot net," said Agent Duncan. "Why's there a dot net subfolder sitting here?"

"For that matter, why's there a Temp folder on the D drive?" asked Jerry. "Look at the creation date—Black Friday. Makes you want to say, 'Hmmm,' doesn't it?"

"Hmmm," said Agent Duncan. "And what's that program file doing there? 'ND45-KB2737084-x86.exe'?"

"Why get so excited by a knowledge base download?" said Ryan. "So what if it's in a weird place. On a busy day like Black Friday, mistakes happen."

"Because nobody's that sloppy," said Jerry.

Ryan was fed up. He walked out of the office to the deli counter in the store. He opened the refrigerator behind the counter and picked up another sandwich. The POS terminal at the front of the store was still on, so he paid for it with cash. He sat down at a table near the front of the store and started eating. Why was he stuck here with these Neanderthals in the middle of the night? He sneezed.

Back in Greta's office: "My money says it's not a program," said Agent Duncan. "Open it with Notepad."

Jerry opened it. They all stared at the screen for a few seconds.

Greta looked at Agent Duncan, then down at Jerry. "What are we looking at?"

"About five hundred credit-card numbers," said Jerry. "This is the consolidation point. All those POS terminals copy their stuff here. They probably just append their records onto the end of this file." He shook his head. "Sloppy move, comrades, very sloppy."

"Huh?" asked Greta.

"Our Russian friends put their loot in the same directory they used for downloading the GreenPOS program to all those POS terminals. That's unwise—they made it easy for us to stumble over it. They should have buried it in another directory and we might not have found it."

Jerry smiled. "We can beat these guys."

"I'm glad you feel confident," said Greta.

"Let's see if we can find their exfiltration vector," said Jerry. "Where do they send this batch of credit-card numbers?"

"Jerry, what's that third file?" asked Agent Duncan, pointing to a file named 'KB2735075-x86.exe' in the same directory. "Open that one with Notepad too."

Jerry opened it. The file had one line that said, "put ND45-KB2737084-x86.exe."

"What's that?" asked Greta.

"FTP," said Jerry. "File Transfer Protocol. That's how you send big files from one computer to another over the Internet. It's especially useful for files that are too big to be email attachments. I'll bet there's a scheduled task on this system that copies those credit-card numbers to Russia."

Agent Duncan said to Jerry, "Let's see the creation date on that file."

Three clicks later, they could all see the date: November 28, 2013.

"That was the Saturday before the banks first noticed the credit-card numbers up for sale from Russia," said Agent Duncan. "Jerry, would you take a screen shot of the directory window to make sure we preserve all the dates on those files?"

After saving the image, Jerry launched the Scheduled Task applet and started exploring.

"I think we found a scheduled task. Another funky name this time, 'Update20131201.' Looks like it runs every day at 4:30 p.m. It does an anonymous upload to an FTP site at IP address 72.21.92.82. Hmm. That doesn't sound Russian."

"Not at all," said Agent Duncan. "What does Whois tell us?"

Jerry launched a web browser and typed http://www.networksolutions.com. He clicked the Whois lookup button and entered 72.21.92.82. "Yup, there it is… Houston, Texas! So it's not Russia, but Houston?"

"Looks like our friends are covering their tracks," said Agent Duncan. "Or maybe we have some bad guys in Texas. I'll get this to the Houston office to track down."

"Wait a minute, what are you telling me?" asked Greta.

"I'm telling you that every day at 4:30 p.m., this server sends a few thousand of your customers' card numbers to a server in Houston," explained Agent Duncan. "We don't know where they end up yet, but we know how to find out."

"We still have some missing pieces of our puzzle here," said Jerry. "I'll do a little more digging."

Greta sat on the sofa in her office while Jerry clicked the RDP session to the store domain controller. "Let's see if we can find our GPO," said Jerry, while Agent Duncan found a coffeemaker in Greta's office and brewed some.

After about an hour, Jerry spoke out. "The plot thickens. I found the GPOs. Looks like our friends compromised two other servers at corporate similar to the one we found. They divided the stores into three sets with each set controlled by one of those compromised 'mother ship' servers. The one we found an hour ago exfiltrates to Houston. Another one goes to Indianapolis and one goes to New Mexico."

"Okay. Call it a night," said Agent Duncan. "Let's pack up and get some sleep."

"Wait a second," said Jerry. "You're just gonna let all those credit-card numbers travel to Russia?"

"Now that we have an idea what's going on," said Agent Duncan, "we need to strategize. For one thing, I don't want to give the Russians advance warning by shutting them down. The best we can do for now is keep track of which numbers are being uploaded and get that to the banks ASAP so they can cancel those cards before the counterfeiters get them. If we can get Bullseye to cooperate."

"They look pretty accommodating right now," said Jerry. Greta was asleep on her sofa and Ryan was snoring with his head down on a table at the front of the store. Drool pooled on the table under his chin.

"Give me just one minute," said Jerry.

"For what?"

"I'm editing my card number outta there."

***

The Wednesday morning sunrise gave the rows of cubicles in the credit-card operations department on the tenth floor of the Uncle Sam Bank building a yellow tint. Director Harlan Phillips's office was in the corner of a row of walled offices along an interior wall. "For the last time, no!" said Harlan, sitting behind his desk. "I should throw you outta here for even suggesting such a thing."

Jesse Jonsen glared across the desk back at Harlan. "And I should walk outta here right now before that Russian sonofabitch owns this bank! Tell ya what—write me a severance check so I can cash it right now before this bank runs out of money!"

Jesse got up from her chair to storm out of Harlan's office. She reached for the office door and tried to turn the handle and wrench the door open. But her timing was off as she pulled on the handle before fully turning it. The door latch hit the strike plate in the doorframe and the door refused to open as the office walls shuddered.

Harlan started to laugh. "Sit down," he said. "Please."

Jesse turned and slumped back into the chair across from Harlan's desk.

"Before you tear apart the flimsy walls in here," said Harlan, "think about what you're doing. You're young and passionate and you're great at your job. That's what we love about you here. But what you're proposing is nuts. Trying to attack this guy with fake credit-card numbers exposes us to all kinds of unknown liability. I don't want to even think about what law enforcement would say if they found out."

"What if I told you the FBI is already on board with this idea?" asked Jesse. "I've already talked it over with Brenda and Lynn and Brenda can get the retired numbers we need."

Harlan leaned back in his chair and stared at Jesse. "You make a lousy poker player."

"Okay, Harlan," said Jesse, "don't say yes yet. Just don't say no. We can make this guy think twice the next time he wants to try this."

Harlan stared at Jesse a few more seconds. "You'll need some programming help to pull this off," said Harlan.

Jesse smiled. "Got it covered."

"I didn't say yes yet," said Harlan. "Now get out of here. I want to hear from your friends at the FBI. And take it easy on my office door."

Operation Lemonade

The Bullseye eleventh floor conference room that Liz Isaacs reserved for the report on the credit-card investigation had large windows overlooking Nicollet Mall. It was nearly 10:00 a.m., and shoppers scurried through the light snow to buy Christmas gifts. Bullseye shoppers had no way of knowing that when they swiped their cards at the checkout counter, their card numbers would make their way to St. Petersburg, Russia.

The soft leather chairs around the oblong mahogany table filled up one by one as the members of the investigative team entered the room and took their seats. At one end of the table was Ryan Mac-Millan, looking groggy. In front of him sat a quart of orange juice and a box of tissues. Liz Isaacs, in a Vera Wang turquoise business suit with a Louis Vuitton raw silk blouse, stood at the door to welcome her guests. The first in was Jesse Jonsen, still wearing her well-worn black blazer, red turtleneck, and blue jeans, followed by Harlan Phillips wearing his usual white shirt with rolled up sleeves and dark tie.

"Jesse! How have you been?" said Liz, as she bent down to give her old colleague a hug and faux kisses near both cheeks. "I can't tell you how much we miss you!"

"You know, I feel just the same way, Liz. I'd like you to meet my manager, Harlan Phillips."

Jesse and Harlan sat down on the opposite end of the table from Ryan.

Jerry Barkley came in next, with Agent Duncan behind him. When Jerry introduced himself, Liz said, "What a remarkable holiday sweater, Mr. Barkley. Is it one of ours?"

"No ma'am. I picked it up at Goodwill last year. It was quite a bargain." Jerry smiled at his lie, but noticed that Liz bit her cheek and winced.

"And Agent Duncan, I hope you're well this morning."

"Yes, ma'am, Ms. Isaacs, ma'am. By the way, did you receive the email I forwarded from Jerry?"

Liz's smile descended into a frown. "Yes, thank you. I'm sure we'll be discussing it."

Agent Duncan and Jerry sat near Jesse, while Liz went to the center of the table and fumbled with the speakerphone. As soon as she achieved a dial tone, she went over to Ryan and gave him a gentle shake on the shoulder, though she appeared to dig her fingernails into him for good measure. He looked hazily across the table at the visitors.

Liz went back near the phone. "I'd like to welcome you here today. As you know, our CEO Mr. Berger is out of the country on important business but agreed to join us by speakerphone today as a gesture of good will and cooperation."

Liz looked at a slip of paper and punched in the phone number, but couldn't get through.

"Ryan, could you look up the country code for Barbados?"

Jesse, Jerry, and Agent Duncan shared a furtive glance, each with a raised eyebrow.

Liz finally got Berger on the speakerphone and introduced everyone.

"Welcome to Bullseye International Headquarters, everyone," said Berger. "I understand the FBI is concerned about a possible security issue?"

"I'm Agent Duncan of the FBI. Thank you, Mr. Berger, for taking the time to meet with us this morning," said Agent Duncan. "Banks across the country report that about thirty million people have had their credit-card numbers stolen and everything points to Bullseye as the source of the leak."

"That's what Liz told me," said Berger. "I find that impossible to believe, but we agreed to cooperate with your investigation."

"The FBI appreciates your cooperation," said Agent Duncan. "First, let's bring everyone up to speed, starting with a report from Jerry Barkley on our forensic investigation at the Lake Street Bullseye last night. Did everyone get Jerry's email?"

"I'll forward it to you right now, Mr. Berger," said Liz, typing on her laptop.

"Mr. Berger, this is Jerry Barkley. I'm in the IT security business on special assignment for Uncle Sam Bank. I wrote down the key points of last night's investigation in some detail in that email. So, I'll just summarize briefly for you now. Basically we observed the data flow in a store by making a credit-card purchase at a checkout counter and we watched the interaction when one of your point-of-sale terminals booted up. We spent several hours analyzing this data and that led us to look at some structural things in your operations."

"Did you verify that credit-card information is being delivered to Russia?" asked Berger.

"Not exactly," said Jerry.

"So all this discussion about a credit-card leak is premature then," said Liz.

"I wouldn't say that," Jerry continued. "We found a nasty program in your point-of-sale system named GreenPOS. It appears to capture credit-card data from each swipe, attach the store's zip code to the file, and then store it in unencrypted form with all the other credit-card numbers from that day of sales. My credit-card number was appended to that file right after I swiped it."

"Agreed, that number should be encrypted," said Liz, "but that still doesn't imply we're sending anything to Russia."

"We didn't find anything going directly to Russia. As I said in the email, the exfiltration path goes from the store to one of three servers at corporate, and then to FTP sites in either Houston, Indianapolis, or New Mexico. We don't know if the people operating those sites are in cahoots with the bad guys, or if they are simply being used."

"We have FBI teams visiting those locations as we speak," chimed in Agent Duncan.

"Our guess," continued Jerry, "is those files are all traveling to Russia. The Russians group them in batches called 'bases' on an underground Russian website."

"Without a definite link to Russia yet," said Liz, "why are you so suspicious of these files you found?"

"For one thing," said Jerry, "the file that contained my credit-card number was given a name to look like a program, when it was actually a document. The obvious conclusion is someone's trying to hide something."

"But I thought we had the best security design in the industry," said Berger. "I understand we have an excellent firewall and antivirus software. How's it even conceivable that somebody could do this?"

"That's right, Mr. Berger," said Ryan. "I designed it myself."

"Your design has a problem," said Jerry, looking at Ryan. "Every store should have its POS systems behind a firewall. All the bad guys had to do was sneak past your main firewall somehow, and then it was easy to infiltrate the computers that run your checkout counters."

Ryan looked more ashen as the conversation continued. "I took the advice of some of the finest consultants in the tech industry when I—er, when we designed that system. Besides, I still haven't heard any definite proof that correlates Bullseye—specifically—with the bogus cards that are showing up on the street.

"I should tell you then about the ten credit cards our bank issued last week," said Jesse.

Over the speakerphone, Berger blurted out, "What cards?"

"We issued ten credit cards last week to certain bank employees across the country," said Jesse. "They each went to their neighborhood Bullseye and bought one item. Then we canceled the cards and put alerts on them. Three phony cards showed up yesterday afternoon, all near the locations where they were first used. The only place they could have possibly come from was Bullseye. They weren't used anywhere else."

Several seconds of silence followed. Jerry looked at Jesse and mouthed, "Wow!" He gave a quiet, respectful nod. Jesse smiled slightly at Jerry.

"Wait a minute," said Ryan. "We don't know where this so-called leak is coming from."

"Yes," said Liz. "How did it get on our internal severs?"

"We don't know yet," said Jerry.

"I'm surprised you haven't gotten any alerts from your security team in Bangalore," said Jesse. "When I worked here, I found they were pretty good at keeping track of any suspicious activity coming in or going out of your system."

"I assure you, our team in Bangalore is watching all those alerts," said Liz. "We spent a lot of money putting all that in place."

"How do they communicate back to corporate?" asked Jerry.

"Email," said Ryan. "They email a group email address and then a member of the security team handles it."

"Okay. Who are the group members?" asked Jerry.

Ryan and Liz looked at each other. "Ummm," said Ryan. "The group name is SecurityOps and we set up Danielle Weyerhauser as the only email group member… Oh, wow! I just remembered Danielle left the company two months ago. She was just an intern and left when we couldn't hire her."

"Why didn't you hire her?" demanded Berger.

"Well, sir," said Liz. "You instituted a hiring freeze for everyone except retail workers."

The room went silent again.

Jerry looked at Ryan and then Liz in disbelief. Ryan looked down. Liz stared straight ahead.

Jesse muttered under her breath, "You mean I was replaced by an intern?"

"So nobody at Bullseye is looking at alerts," said Agent Duncan after several tense seconds. "Which means, for the past two months, at least, any email to the SecurityOps group from the team in India disappeared into a black hole. You spent a lot of money to put a system in place and then you didn't use it. I suggest you resurrect the last year of messages from Bangalore for analysis. We have a team coming in from Quantico eager to take a look."

Liz started to protest but Berger cut her off. "Why don't we hold off on assigning blame for now and focus on minimizing the damage and protecting Bullseye customers?"

"An excellent idea, sir," said Ryan.

"All I can say," said Liz, "is that if somebody broke into our system, it must have been a highly sophisticated operation."

"No," said Jerry. "They messed up, which made it easy for us to find their GreenPOS program. They put it in the same folder where they collected stolen card data. They're not that sophisticated. We can beat 'em."

"So what's our next step?" asked Berger.

Harlan Looked at Jesse. Jesse looked at Agent Duncan. "We have more."

The whole room turned to Jesse, now ready for the next shock.

"We have an idea," said Jesse. "Carders work by reputation. Carders with reputations for the cleanest dumps make the most money, so they guard their reputations jealously."

"I think I see where you're going with this," said Jerry, "and I like it."

"Dumps?" asked Berger over the speakerphone.

"A dump is a credit-card record," said Jesse. "Sorry—my alter ego, Teena Fay from Green Bay, deals with these guys all the time and I slip into their language. Anyway," she said, looking at Jerry, "since you guys found the trail to Russia last night, I think we can fill that trail with a few million bogus card numbers. Maybe we can hammer this guy's reputation and cost him some money."

"We're not in a position to turn our whole IT network into your playground," said Liz.

Ignoring Liz and glancing at Harlan, Jesse continued. "I'm supposed to get official permission from the FBI to collaborate with other banks and credit-card companies on this. So say yes and let's make some lemonade out of this lemon."

Agent Duncan leaned back in his chair and looked at Jesse. After a few seconds, a slight grin formed on his lips and a twinkle appeared in his eyes. The grin slowly turned into a wide smile. He nodded slightly a few times, leaned forward, and said, "I don't have the authority to say yes, but I'll call my boss and I'll bet I can have a yes for you this afternoon." Now looking at Harlan and smiling, he said, "Harlan, I'll have my boss call you. Since he had an issue with his ATM card after he shopped at a Bullseye last week, I don't think it'll be a problem."

Over the speakerphone, Daniel asked, "What would a project like this entail and what would it cost?"

Agent Duncan looked at Jesse, then Jerry. "Let's find out where the trail leads and then test the feasibility of Jesse's suggestion."

"Wait a minute!" said Liz. "We're a retail store, not some spy agency."

Now turning to Liz, Agent Duncan continued, "And if you go along with this, Bullseye Stores will have the personal good will of some higher-ups with the United Stated Federal Bureau of Investigation. That might be valuable when a blogger somewhere publishes this story sooner or later."

And to Jesse, Agent Duncan asked, "How would this work?"

"As you know," said Jesse, "credit-card numbers are sixteen digits. The first six digits of every credit-card number is called a BIN, or Bank Identification Number. That leaves ten digits, or 9,999,000,000 possible card numbers for each BIN, give or take. Every issuer will have a bucket of used, canceled, and available numbers. Every time anyone changes cards for any reason, that old number goes into the bucket. By now, there are millions of numbers in those buckets—we just put ten numbers in ours last week. So I'm proposing we work with the other banks and issuers and borrow some of those numbers to burn our friend's reputation. He calls himself Tarman, by the way. So don't plug the leak right away. First, let's pour some sour lemonade through it. Maybe he'll think twice before doing this again."

"Lemonade?" asked Ryan, looking at his orange juice.

"Exactly," said Jerry. "When life gives you lemons…"

Jesse smiled. "So Harlan, how about it?"

Harlan sat back in his chair and looked at everyone in the group. Jesse, Jerry, and Agent Duncan met his gaze. Liz looked away. Ryan looked down at his hands. "Jesse, you're nuts. You guys are all nuts. Make this happen. I'll sell it upstairs. Maybe somebody will write a book about all this someday."

"Okay. Project Lemonade it is," said Agent Duncan. "Jerry, what do you need?"

"Just get me those credit-card numbers," said Jerry. "I'll whip up some scripts. This should be fun."

Team Lemonade poured ten million sour numbers through the digital pipeline to Russia between Wednesday and Sunday. It was exhilarating.

But nothing lasts forever.

Power of the Press

The only visual the public ever saw of blogger and former newspaper reporter Henry Lincoln was the small headshot he published on his website. It was a picture of an African-American with a confident smile and a twinkle in his eye. That's all anyone needed to see because Henry wrote stories about the dark side of the Internet and had more than his share of enemies.

Something was up this Monday morning—Henry could almost smell it. A character named Tarman was offering millions of credit cards for sale on the underground Linoza.so website and it was buzzing with posts.

Henry joined Linoza.so several months earlier and found himself logging in every day to keep up with what was going on. Of course, Henry used a fake identity on this site. Here, his name was a simple 'helola' registered with a free Hotmail email address.

Reading through the posts, speculation was rampant. Where did these dumps come from? Maybe Tarman hacked a bank. Or maybe he hacked a credit-card processor and stole all the card numbers. Others suggested he penetrated an ATM network. But everybody agreed on one thing: Tarman was a hero. The comments sections of his posts were filled with hundreds of compliments and offers to buy stolen credit-card numbers from him.

"They're all sick," said Henry to himself as he read post after post extolling the virtues of this hacker society and their current hero, the mystery character named Tarman. "Nothing more than high-tech groupies and crooks."

This was big. After a couple days of this, somebody somewhere had to know the origin for all these credit-card numbers. As an award-winning veteran investigative reporter, Henry knew how to find things out, and this story could blow the lid off of something.

Henry called a friend in the fraud department at Metropolis Bank. "Hey Jennie, this is Henry. What's going on with those credit-card numbers on Linoza.so?"

"Hello to you, too, Henry. Didn't I tell you not to call this number unless it's an emergency?"

"Okay, consider this an emergency. You're looking at the same bases I am. Where are they coming from?"

"I really can't comment."

"Okay, don't comment. Just tell your friend, where are they coming from?"

"Henry, you know good and well I can't do that. If I did, I would have a… bullseye… on my back."

"Huh?"

"Look, Henry, I'm not telling you anything, okay? Let's just say that if you used a credit card at a Bullseye recently, you should probably have it cancelled and get a new one. Okay?"

"You're kidding!"

"Listen, I gotta go."

"See ya. And thanks. I owe you one."

"You owe me more than one, Henry."

Henry dialed another number, this one a private line to a friend at Pursuit Bank.

"Hey, Terri—I heard a rumor that all those new bases up for sale on Linoza.so came from Bullseye Stores. Is it true?"

"How do you find this stuff?"

"It's what I do. I just can't stop pursuing truth. That's why I talk to people like you, with knowledge."

"You didn't hear anything from me, okay? Henry, this is big. Some of my managers are talking about billions in potential liabilities."

"Thanks, Terri."

"You owe me lunch."

"Next time I'm in town, I'll pay up."

"Well, all I can say is, you better feed me before I feed you any more confidential information."

"I'll be making reservations soon."

One more call to make. Henry heard a cheery recorded message. "This is the Bullseye Corporate Communication Office. If you know your party's extension …"

Henry listened to the electronic greeting and pressed 6 for Media Relations.

"Hi, Brittany Chatsworth, Corporate Communications. How may I help you?"

"Hi, Brittany. My name is Henry Lincoln, a reporter for *Lincoln on Security* blog."

"Okay…"

"I'm not sure if we've met. I do investigative reporting on IT security issues. That also used to be my beat when I was with the *Washington Post*."

"Oh, my. How impressive!"

"I'm calling because I heard Bullseye is dealing with a major data breach. I know that it's millions of names, but I'm not sure how many millions. I'm wondering if you'd line up an interview with your CIO—and your CEO, while you're at it. I noticed you haven't put out a news release yet. Were you just waiting to do a news conference?"

"Um, Mr. Lincoln, would you please hold for just one minute?"

"Sure."

The line went silent. "I must have touched a nerve," thought Henry. "I could hear her sweat."

After a few minutes, another voice came on the line, sounding tense.

"Hello, Mr. Lincoln. This is Liz Isaacs, the CIO for Bullseye. How may I help you?"

"Hi, Liz! Thank you for taking the time to speak with me. I'm doing a story on your data breach and would like to give you the opportunity to comment. Would it be possible to do a phone interview? I anticipate it'll take about a half hour."

"I'm sorry, Mr. Lincoln, I'm not familiar with your publication. Would you mind telling me who you work for?"

"Of course. My website is LincolnOnSecurity.com."

"I see. Unfortunately, as a policy, we're unable to comment on ongoing investigations. But thank you for your call. Is there anything else I can help you with?"

"Yes. Is that Liz, L-I-Z? And Isaacs, I-S-A-A-C-S?"

"Yes, that's right. May I ask, when do you plan to release this story?"

"I should have something up tonight; that's why I really need to talk with you."

"Thank you, Mr. Lincoln."

"Call me Henry. Thank you for your time, Liz."

So it was true. And Henry had the scoop. Somehow, somebody stole millions of credit-card numbers from this company and was selling them in an underground website. Yup, this was big.

***

The email from the CEO's office went out later that day. Agent Duncan forwarded a copy to Jesse and Jerry.

From: Brittany Chatsworth for Daniel Berger
Sent: Monday, December 16, 2013 3:04 PM
To: Liz Isaacs; Ryan MacMillan; Connor Duncan
Cc: bullseye-BOD; bullseye-employees
Subject: Operation Lemonade

I want to personally thank Liz Isaacs and Ryan MacMillan with the Bullseye IT department, who conceived and led a heroic effort we named "Operation Lemonade" to repel a sophisticated cyberattack from a well-funded Russian organized criminal gang against our system.

Liz Isaacs informed me earlier today that she took a call from an Internet blogger named Henry Lincoln this morning. Lincoln writes a blog about Internet security and plans to publish what he knows about the attack later this evening. Unfortunately, this means we must immediately terminate Operation Lemonade.

We will provide more details on the Bullseye website. Watch for a press release in the next few days.

Regards,
Daniel Berger
Office of the CEO
Bullseye Stores

***

With Project Lemonade shut down, the focus turned toward dismantling the system.

"Hey, Jerry," said Agent Duncan. "Have you dug anything up yet about the original source of the leak?"

"Yeah," said Jerry. "I think we're onto something. Looking in the security data logs, we found a user, ERousseau, logging in at all hours of the night last spring. And the source IP addresses were always in St. Petersburg, Russia. The Bullseye IT department helped us track down her username. It belongs to a plumbing contractor in upstate New York. And then Liz and Ryan led a heroic effort to change her password."

Agent Duncan smiled. "Send me specifics on that contractor and I'll have somebody go talk to them."

"What's up with our three external FTP servers?" asked Jerry.

"I saw an email from the Albuquerque office a few minutes ago," said Agent Duncan. "They called Fool's Gold Academy, and in the spirit of our Lemonade operation, they might turn the lessons they're learning from this whole affair into a semester class. And in Indianapolis—that guy was a vet. Some sort of gamer. He offered to fly over to Russia and punch out our buddy, Tarman. Tomorrow they're showing him how to lock down his FTP site. And Houston's sending a couple of agents for a call Wednesday morning."

Shutting Down the Pipeline

The 8:00 a.m. temperature in Houston, Texas, was a chilly forty-five degrees on Wednesday, December 18th. Lloyd Wright's mood was even chillier as he rode to the office of Wright Design with his dad, Frank Wright. After a grueling fall sophomore semester in college, Lloyd wanted Christmas break to actually provide a break. But Frank Wright wanted Lloyd in the office. People were complaining about slow computers and Lloyd, as the family computer expert, was the man to fix it. The $200 from Dad was nice, but a break from work would have been nicer.

After arriving at the office, Lloyd looked for Wendy Stevens, the young, brunette receptionist with the nice, um, smile. "Yeah, that was it," Lloyd lied to himself. She had a nice smile and a great personality and Lloyd wondered what her hair would look like if she let it down from the bun she always wore. Well, it was as good a place to start as any.

"Hi, Wendy," said Lloyd. "Dad asked me to look at some computers this morning."

"Well, good morning, Lloyd!" said Wendy. "Coming into work on your college break—that's so sweet!"

"Um, well, yeah, I guess," said Lloyd, his mood turning warmer. "Thanks! So what's going on with your computer?"

"Well, it's just slow, that's all," said Wendy. "Like when I send an email; it takes forever to get there. And it takes forever for emails to get to me. I even tested it with one of our suppliers. He was trying to email some specs to me while we were on the phone and it took almost ten minutes for his email to get here. Sometimes, other people in the office don't even get their emails from customers."

"The whole Internet's slow," continued Wendy. "Here, let me show you." She launched a web browser and Wendy and Lloyd stared at the screen for almost sixty seconds until a window popped up with a simple search field.

"Just a minute, sweetie," said Wendy as the phone rang. "Good morning, Wright Design." A pause. "Could you hold for just one second, please?"

Wendy pressed the intercom button on her phone and Frank's extension. "Frank? I know y'all haven't had your morning coffee yet, but I think you might want to take this."

She transferred the call to Frank and turned to Lloyd with a troubled look.

"What is it?" asked Lloyd.

"That was the FBI," she whispered. "Now why do you suppose they're calling here?"

Wendy and Lloyd went back to work on Wendy's computer. The computer seemed okay, but interactions with the Internet were intolerable.

Frank Wright appeared outside of his office in the back. "Lloyd, could I see you in my office, please?"

Lloyd looked at Wendy, curious. Wendy mouthed silently, "I don't know. But you better get back there."

"What's wrong?" asked Lloyd, as Frank closed the door.

"The FBI wants our help tracking down some things on the Internet," said Frank.

"What?"

"The FBI guy said he wants our help. He said he'd be here in an hour and he wants to meet with my IT department. That's you. So what's going on?"

"I don't know, Dad. I have no idea what they want."

Lloyd walked out of his dad's office, shaken and afraid as thoughts raced through his mind.

"What could the FBI possibly want? What am I worried about? Oh crap, that's gotta be it! All that music! That music-sharing service! That's gotta be what they're after!"

Visions of a shadowy room with a swinging bare lightbulb filled his head.

He tried to look composed while walking away from his dad's office. But instead of going to his desk, he turned and walked into the men's room. He splashed water on his face as a wave of nausea started below his stomach and worked its way up to his throat.

A plan started to form as he fought the nausea. Maybe the FBI or the NSA or some other spook agency was watching all the Internet traffic in and out of here, but if they didn't find anything when they arrived, maybe they would be willing to make a deal. Yeah, that could work. He could be the small fish in a big pond. Dad would be mad, but he would deal with that later.

Lloyd composed himself and walked out of the men's room to his cubicle and logged on his computer. First things first, he thought, as he clicked "Control Panel… Programs and Features" and removed the music-sharing software. He clicked "Yes" when it asked if he also wanted to delete all his songs—11,735 songs collected over three years, all gone. After a reboot, he navigated to the directory where the software stored his music and emptied all of it by hand, then removed the directory.

The FBI could still read deleted files though. He'd heard that someplace. A tour through a search engine showed several programs he could download to clean up deleted files. He found one for ninety-nine dollars, downloaded it, and ran it. With any luck, it would finish before the FBI arrived.

Aw, nuts! The backups! He had backup copies on the server! He launched Remote Desktop in another window and logged onto the server. He quickly navigated to the directory with his music backups and deleted it. But now another problem—what to do about deleted files on the server? Another ninety-nine dollars and another download would take care of that.

Lloyd watched as the percent-complete bar graphs on the server and his workstation slowly grew. It was a race—the software had to finish before the FBI got here. But what if it didn't? Well it just would, that's all.

The server said 30 percent complete after thirty minutes. Not looking good.

Fifty percent complete after forty-five minutes. Time for plan B. Click the "Cancel" button—maybe it wiped those backup files already even though it didn't finish all of it. Canceling…

It was still canceling ten minutes later as two men wearing suits walked in the front door and up to the front desk.

Out of time! Click the red X. "This program has become unresponsive. If you close the program, you might lose information." Two choices: "Close the program" or "Wait for the program to respond."

Lloyd clicked "Close the program" and the whole Remote Desktop session froze. A few seconds later, a small window popped up that said, "The connection has been lost. Attempting to reconnect to your session. Connection attempt: 1 of 20."

The suits were talking to Wendy. Wendy pressed her intercom button. The phone rang in Frank's office.

Connection attempt: 2 of 20.

He could hear Frank. "I'll be right up."

The designer in the next cubicle popped his head up. "Hey Lloyd, where's my 'T' drive?"

Connection attempt: 3 of 20.

"Um, not sure. Let me take a look." Lloyd clicked "Start… Computer" from his own workstation. The free-space cleaner still running on Lloyd's workstation was 60 percent done. Lloyd tried to navigate to his "T" drive. It hung. "Looks like a server issue. I'll go check it out."

Lloyd stood up and began walking to the server closet, where the server sat on a temporary, dusty plywood shelf supported by some two-by-fours surrounding file cabinets that stored old blueprints from long-forgotten projects. He would need to connect a monitor to the server and find out what was going on. And he'd need a ladder so he could reach the back of the server to connect the monitor. Maybe one of the designers was out on a job site and he could borrow the monitor from the designer's computer. Hopefully a ladder would be handy in the janitor closet.

Frank met Lloyd in the cubicle isle. "The FBI's here. Let's go."

"I'll be right there," said Lloyd. "Server issue."

"It can wait," said Frank. "Come on."

Lloyd looked down at his monitor. Connection attempt 7 of 20. The free-space cleaner on his workstation said 62 percent complete.

Connection attempt: 8 of 20.

"Dad, wait. I need to tell you something."

Frank looked at him.

"Dad, I've been sharing music. They want me." That nauseous feeling was coming again.

"*What?*"

"I've been downloading music and sharing it for three years. That's why they're here."

"How do you know?"

"Why else would they be here?"

"I don't know, but I don't think the FBI cares if you download music. Now come on!"

"I have to go to the bathroom," said Lloyd as he ran from his cubicle towards the men's room to throw up.

Connection attempt: 12 of 20 popped up on Lloyd's screen. The free-space cleaner showed 65 percent complete.

Frank looked down at Lloyd's computer with no idea what was going on. Figuring that out would have to wait. Hopefully, Lloyd would pull himself together.

Frank shook his head and walked up to the front desk. He flashed a smile and offered a handshake. "Hi, I'm Frank Wright."

The tall one with thinning hair introduced himself as Roland Harper. The other young one was Beau Hamilton.

To Wendy, Frank said, "Lloyd is, um, busy for just a minute. When he comes up, would you send him to the conference room?"

"Will do," said Wendy.

Frank, Roland, and Beau walked around the corner and disappeared into the conference room.

Ten minutes later, Lloyd walked up to the front desk.

"Lloyd, honey, you look awful," said Wendy. "Are you sick?"

"I'm not sure," said Lloyd. "Maybe."

"Well, your dad said to tell you they're right over there in the conference room and he wants you in there," said Wendy. "But goodness sakes, we have to make you presentable!"

Wendy took a hairbrush from her purse and straightened Lloyd's hair. "Nancy, would you watch the phones for just a minute for me?" Wendy asked one of designers.

Wendy guided Lloyd back to the employee break room, poured some water into a Styrofoam cup, and told Lloyd to take a few sips. Lloyd sipped the water, swished it around in his mouth, and spat it out in the sink. "Thanks, Wendy. I'll be fine," he mumbled. But he wouldn't be fine. He was on his way to prison. He hugged Wendy, wiped the tears from his eyes with a tissue, and started the long journey down the hallway to the reception desk.

As he walked past his cubicle, he saw two windows on his computer monitor. "The remote desktop connection has failed," in one window, and "71 percent complete" in the other.

"Face it like a man." Isn't that what Dad always said? "No matter what it is, face it like a man." Well, that's what he would do. He grabbed two tissues from his cubicle. He blew his nose with one and wiped the tears from his face with the other. He would survive. He tossed the tissues in the trash and continued walking.

At the receptionist desk, he turned left. He was sure all eyes in the office were on him by now. He could hear people quietly talk about him as he turned towards the conference room.

As he walked by the receptionist desk, Nancy looked up and wondered, "What's wrong with Lloyd?" The designers were now able to access their "T" drive as the server finished rebooting. Other than Wendy and Nancy, nobody noticed Lloyd's private perp walk through the office.

"What's wrong with Lloyd?" asked Nancy as Wendy returned to the reception desk.

"I surely don't know," said Wendy. "He looked fine a few minutes ago. Maybe it's the stomach flu."

Lloyd walked into the conference room and found Frank and the two suits talking. Frank looked up. "Lloyd, come on in. This is Roland Harper and Beau Hamilton." Lloyd mumbled something, shook hands with both men, and sat down. Face it like a man. Face it like a man.

"Look, Mr. Harper, Mr. Hamilton—I'm the guy you want. My dad had nothing to do with any of this."

Beau and Roland looked at each other. "Okay," said Roland.

"It was my fault. I signed up three years ago. It didn't seem like anything harmful, but listen, I was only seventeen. But I've kept it up since then—you guys already know that—so I'm ready to face the music. I'm twenty years old now. I'm an adult. I shouldn't have done it."

"Son, just what in the *hell* are you talking about?" boomed Frank.

"Dad, I just told you. I've been sharing music for three years. That's why these guys are here!"

Roland and Beau looked at each other again. "Um, Lloyd, are you freely admitting you illegally downloaded and shared music?" asked Beau.

"Yes," said Lloyd.

Frank's face turned red.

"Okay," said Beau. "We can, um, deal with that later."

"As we were explaining to your dad," said Roland, "we're looking for your help tracking down some interactions with Russia."

"Son," said Frank, "what's an FTP site?"

"Huh?" asked Lloyd, trying to comprehend what was happening. Maybe he wasn't going to prison?

"It's a simple enough question," said Frank. "What's an FTP site?"

"That's what we use to share drawings with customers," said Lloyd. "Remember, we set it up last summer. Designers save the drawings in the "P" drive, and they call the customers to download them."

Lloyd paused. "But wait a minute," he said. "You guys didn't come here because of my music sharing?"

Beau and Roland looked at each other again.

"No," said Beau. "We didn't. But now that you've admitted to illegal activity, we'll have to handle that too."

"Yeah, sure, anything," said Lloyd.

Frank chuckled, shook his head, and laughed. His eyes started to water as he laughed louder. He wiped his eyes and shook his head again.

"What?" asked Lloyd.

"Son, these men don't give a rat's rear-end about your music sharing. You'll answer to me for that later. But for now, let's just give these men what they want, okay? Apparently, we're helping somebody send credit-card numbers to Russia and I think it would be a good idea to put a stop to that."

Lloyd stared at Frank, dumbfounded. Then he looked at Roland and Beau. "You guys don't care about music sharing?"

"Well, we care, yes," said Beau. "But the recording industry cares more."

"I understand the judgments are in the five or six figures when they press lawsuits," said Roland. "There was a case recently in northern Minnesota. Tell ya what. You help us track down what we're looking for and we'll forget you told us anything about sharing music. Deal?"

"Absolutely!" said Lloyd.

"Good. We need to look at your server logs to find out who's been uploading and downloading things from your FTP site. Somebody must have guessed your password or compromised your server somehow."

"We don't have any passwords on the site," said Lloyd. "We wanted to make it easy for our customers."

"Well, that explains it," said Roland. "You do realize if your customers can log on anonymously, so can anyone else in the world."

"But they have to know we're here first," said Lloyd.

"You'd be surprised how fast the Russians can find you," said Roland.

"The Russians?" asked Frank.

"Yeah," said Roland. "And if the information we have is correct, they moved something like ten million credit-card numbers through here over the past few days."

"Do you think that could slow down our computers?" asked Lloyd.

"So that's what that was all about," said Frank. "If we're part of somebody's credit-card scam, I'd like you to show my son how to shut it down. And Lloyd, I'll talk to you later."

By lunchtime, the men from the FBI had what they needed, and more. In addition to moving credit-card numbers, the Wright Design FTP site was also the unwitting host for an international child porn ring. The Internet was slow because lowlifes around the world moved gigabytes of pictures and video in and out of the Wright Design FTP site all day long. Using IP addresses gathered from the logs, the FBI would eventually help law enforcement agencies around the world arrest and prosecute the ringleaders.

Lloyd Wright never recovered his songs. But he learned how to disable anonymous FTP uploads and the value of professional IT services.

Lemonade & Vodka Coolers

"ERousseau, what have you done?" moaned Yuri. "We had such a good relationship, while it lasted." The flow of incoming credit-card numbers had suddenly stopped the day before, and all access attempts to any of the three US-based FTP sites failed with "Access denied" errors. The log-in credentials for ERousseau no longer worked. Neither did the administrative-level account he set up. It was over.

But it was glorious while it lasted. Forty million credit-card numbers were his. At an average selling price of thirty US dollars each, Yuri would have more than one billion US dollars. How many rubles was that? Too many to count!

All that was left was to finish selling them on Linoza.so. Even at one million dumps per day, he would have to post a new base every day for a month to work through it all.

Perhaps he would use two million dumps per base. They would no doubt lose value quickly now that Bullseye had shut off the data flow; especially if somehow the break-in was publicized. But it was doubtful anyone would do that—too embarrassing.

Millions were already in Yuri's bank account, but it was not enough. It would never be enough.

Trouble in Russia

Fyodor Renkin was concerned. Linoza.so was suddenly filling up with posts complaining that Tarman's dumps were no good. Not just one or two dumps, but entire bases. And yet that mama's boy kept offering more bases for sale under Ivan's name. The Proconsul, now becoming a ripper? It would be devastating for business. It had to stop.

"Yuri Makerov is no longer useful. And now he brings shame on my community by selling worthless dumps! It's time to pay him a visit, and to take what is rightfully mine."

***

The message waiting for Yuri in Tarman's private Linoza.so inbox the next morning was chilling and brief:

```
"You will meet me near where the cars are
parked behind the Ibis Centre Hotel. 2 AM. Be
there or Ivan Tarski's killers will find you
next. The Ibis Centre is a special place, is it
not?"
```

The message was unsigned. Somebody in the Linoza.so society knew about Ivan and Yuri's escape from death with his family. But who?

How? Yuri could see only one way to find out. Of course, he would be careful. With a five-month-pregnant fiancé, he had to be careful.

Shortly after midnight, Yuri approached the Ibis from the South along Ligovsky Avenue. He left his car a block from the hotel. He walked past the Ibis front entrance, and turned right into the alley. He saw the parking lot and a few cars.

Now a decision: continue in the open toward the cars, leaving the relative safety of the shadow of the hotel building, or stay in the shadow and watch? Staying in the shadow was the right choice. Still ninety minutes early.

Suddenly, a bright white light blinded him. Just as quickly, it was gone. He could see nothing but an afterimage. He heard footsteps approaching from a different direction than the light.

"Stay where you are, Yuri Makerov," said a voice. "You're early. Why do you impersonate Ivan Tarski on my website? And why does a mama's boy pretend to be a man?"

"And who are you?" asked Yuri. "Fyodor?"

A bullet whizzed by Yuri's ear. Curious, no gun sound.

"I'll ask the questions. Why do you impersonate Tarski on my website?"

"Because Ivan is dead," said Yuri. "Killed while trying to kill my family and me."

"So your murdered my Proconsul. Why do you dishonor my website by presenting worthless merchandise?" asked the voice.

"It's not worthless," said Yuri. "It was obtained at great cost. Are you…?"

"I hold the rank of Caesar. I tolerate much, but will not tolerate anyone violating the honor of Linoza.so. I find you guilty," said the voice.

"Guilty?" asked Yuri. "Of what?"

"End this," said another voice. Familiar. No! This could not be her!

The second bullet struck Yuri between the eyes. He was dead before his body hit the ground.

Fyodor walked under a dim light. "He was not worthy of you, my love. But he served his purpose. He made us rich beyond belief."

Oksana put down the spotlight. The two entered Fyodor's Mercedes, shared a passionate kiss, and slowly drove away, as if nothing had happened.

"Fyodor, did you pick up the tickets yet? When is our flight? I can't wait to feel the warmth of the beaches of Brazil."

"My darling, why be in such a rush? We'll have our whole life together."

"You didn't buy them, did you?"

"Dear Oksana, I have many business dealings that need to be settled before I leave. Be patient. And my oldest son has his first hockey game next month."

"What about *our* son?"

Fyodor pretended he didn't hear her.

"Tell me, Fyodor, do you promise to go away with me before our child is born?"

"Yes, I promise. I swear on my heart."

"Oh, Fyodor! You make me so happy! Please pull over by this park so we can toast the beginning of our life together."

"My love, you think of everything," said Fyodor.

Oksana grabbed her bag out of the backseat and pulled out a bottle of champagne and two glasses. She filled both glasses.

"They say a few sips won't hurt my baby."

Fyodor took a long swig from his glass. Oksana put the glass to her lips, but did not touch the liquid.

Suddenly, Fyodor clutched at his chest, gasping for air.

Oksana took the glass from Fyodor's hand and stepped out of the car. With a sympathetic voice, she said, "Poison, I'm afraid. You won't last a minute."

Fyodor's legs stretched out and he pushed back on the seat. He leaned toward the open door, and with his last breath he asked, "Why?"

"Because, my love, our son deserves a life away from all this. And now he shall have it."

Oksana carefully poured the poison champagne onto the grass, put the glasses into her bag, closed the car door, and quickly walked away.

Fyodor's arm went up for an instant, and then he collapsed on the steering wheel. The sound of his blaring horn pierced the still evening.

***

After a short train ride, Oksana was back at her apartment. She tried to be quiet so Sofia wouldn't hear her. So far, so good. She went to Yuri's laptop to arrange plane tickets. She just needed to get away quickly; she didn't care where. She saw a flight to Greece leaving in an hour from the St. Petersburg airport. "Great, I'll buy it." But when she clicked the button to make the payment, her check card was rejected. "Inadequate balance? But that can't be. I know Yuri put a fortune in there." She quickly checked the balance and screamed out loud when she saw all the zeroes.

"Oksana, is that you?" called Sofia from her room.

"Yes, Sofia. Sorry to bother you. I just saw a mouse."

"Poor dear, let me help you." Sofia rolled into the living room, holding a pistol in her right hand.

Oksana's eyes opened widely when she saw the gun. "It was just a small mouse. You don't need to shoot it."

"Where's my Yuri?"

"He won't be back till late."

"Where is he?"

"I don't know."

"Then how do you know he'll be back late?"

"I, uh…"

"Going somewhere? You're dressed for traveling. And your bag is packed."

"I was… uhh… Do you know what happened to Yuri's account? All my money… his money?"

"Oh, I see. It's always about money. Well, I have it. Yuri was very worried when he left tonight. I told him to take a gun but he said he could handle it. The last thing he did was transfer all his money to my account, 'just in case.'"

"You old worm! That was my money! I need it for—your grandchild!"

"Let's not kid ourselves. We both know Yuri was not the father of your child. Don't think I didn't see how your attitude changed every time you went to visit your 'mother.' You might have fooled Yuri, but you never fooled me."

"Damn you, old woman! That's right, Yuri is dead. His body's lying lifeless in some parking lot, and I helped set him up!"

"The truth at last, my little Oksana," said Sofia as she lifted the pistol and took aim. "Get out of my home before I kill you like you killed my son."

Oksana quickly grabbed her bag and hurried out the door, slamming it loudly. Sofia wheeled to the door and locked it.

She took a breath, looked down, and started crying, softly.

Full Circle

A well-dressed stranger walked into Rousseau Plumbing and Mechanical.

"Hello, may I help you?"

"Good morning. I'm Agent Martin Langer from the FBI. I'm looking for Max and Edith Rousseau."

"I'm Edith. Do you want me to get Max?"

"Yes, I'd like to talk to both of you," said Agent Langer.

Edith led the agent to Max's office. Agent Langer said, "I'll get right to the point. Edith, you noticed your password into the Bullseye network changed recently?"

"Yes, it did," said Edith. "They told me they needed to change it because of a security issue. How did you know that?"

"There's more to it," said Agent Langer "You'll hear about this on the news over the next few days. We thought you should hear it privately from us first. You were the security issue."

"What?!" asked Max.

"Somebody used Edith's password to steal around forty million credit-card numbers," said Agent Langer. "Nobody knows how much money this breach will cost, but the numbers we've heard are in the billions."

"Wait a minute," said Max. "We're a small contractor. We work on plumbing for refrigeration systems. The only reason we even log into that system is to get paid. And that's their rules, not ours."

"I realize that," said Agent Langer. "Have either of you been to Russia recently?"

"Russia?!" asked Max.

"That's where the log-ins came from. Somebody in Russia used your credentials to go much deeper into the Bullseye network than the payment system."

"Are you here to arrest us?" asked Max.

"I'm guessing neither of you have been to Russia recently," said Agent Langer.

"Of course not," said Max.

"Listen," said Agent Langer. "If we thought you were stealing credit cards, we would approach you differently. Max, if you want to contact an attorney, you're free to do so. And it might even be a good idea because you'll probably hear from the media soon. But from the FBI point of view, you're not in any legal trouble."

"How did they get my password in Russia?" asked Edith.

"That's what I'm hoping to find out," said Agent Langer. "When was the last time you did a virus scan on your computer?"

"I don't know," said Edith. "What's a virus scan?"

"Would it be okay if I ran one now?" asked Agent Langer.

"Be my guest," said Max. "I was going to get her a new computer after Christmas and have my son set it up."

"What antivirus software do you use?" asked Agent Langer.

"You'll have to ask my son. He's the one who always wants me to spend more money on that stuff," said Max. "But this whole thing is a racket."

"Well, it's a good idea to protect yourself," said Agent Langer.

"It's not like we keep national security secrets here," said Max. "We don't have anything in any of our computers anyone else would care about."

"Apparently, you do," said Agent Langer.

"And what would that be?" asked Max.

"Well, for one, the password to get inside Bullseye's network," said Agent Langer.

"So you're telling me that somebody stole that password from Edith's computer and used it to steal credit cards?" asked Max.

"Yes, that's exactly what I'm telling you," said Agent Langer. "Forty million of them. You weren't the only link, but you were the first link in the chain."

"So how did they do it?" asked Max.

"Probably with malware," said Agent Langer.

"Malware—yeah, that's the stuff Jerome said we need to install," said Edith. "He's my son."

Agent Langer smiled. "Probably Malwarebytes. That's a free program to clean malware. Malware—short for malicious software. Malwarebytes isn't a complete solution, but it's better than not having anything."

"Well, I'm not spending any more money to turn off parts of the Internet," said Max. "I'm running a business, not a cash drain."

"May I ask you a question?" asked Agent Langer.

"Yeah, sure," said Max.

"Do you have a lock on your front door?" asked Agent Langer.

"Yeah," said Max. "Back door too."

"How about your car? Your house? Do you lock those doors?" asked Agent Langer.

"Yeah, of course," said Max.

"Why?" asked Agent Langer.

"That's a ridiculous question," said Max. "To keep crooks out."

"It's just common sense, right?" asked Agent Langer.

"Yeah," said Max.

"So why leave your Internet front door wide open?" asked Agent Langer.

"Jerome says we have a firewall, so our Internet front door isn't wide open," said Edith.

"Maybe not," said Agent Langer. "But on the Internet, you have a front door, several side doors, and maybe a few back doors. Just because you block the obvious front door doesn't mean you have all the other doors covered. And just like there are crooks out on the streets, there are crooks all over the Internet."

"And I'm a small fish in a big pond," said Max. "Nobody cares about me."

"Apparently somebody in Russia cares about us," said Edith. "I feel terrible!"

"Max, let me address that," said Agent Langer. "It's true. Most of the time, you don't have anything worth stealing. But stealing from you isn't the goal. The goal is to use you to help steal from somebody else. And there are lots of clever ways to enlist your help. That's the real racket out there."

"So what do I do about it?" asked Max.

"For starters, bring in a commercial antivirus solution. And keep your systems patched, especially anything that touches the Internet," said Agent Langer. "And be vigilant. You're the last and best line of defense keeping malicious activity out of here."

"That all costs money," said Max. "Where's the ROI?"

"Yup, it probably costs a few hundred dollars," said Agent Langer.

"I'll think about it," said Max.

"Do more than think about it," said Agent Langer. "The bad publicity from this incident alone will cost you more than any credible IT security solution. That's your ROI."

January Golf

Mike Swanson, senior vice president of operations at Uncle Sam Bank in Minneapolis, could not have been more pleased with Jesse Jonsen and the contractor she had found. Mike still wasn't sure how she plucked this guy out of nowhere, but he came through when needed. And even though there was no way to tell what those fake credit-card numbers did to the Russian crooks, Jesse provided some clues when she found the fake credit-card numbers up for sale one day, and then the seller just disappeared the next day and never came back. Now these crooks knew they had messed with the wrong bank.

He was finally able to reschedule his Miami golf vacation for the week after the New Year. A bear of a man at six-foot-four and 275 pounds, he looked out of place with his close-cropped dark hair, bright green shorts, pale white legs, Hawaiian shirt, and golf shoes, but it was Florida in January and he was determined to enjoy it with his wife. And as a bonus, family friend Henri Carpentier also happened to be in Miami that week with his wife to attend a board meeting with one of his companies. When both men figured out they would be in the same city at the same time with their wives, and the tee time was available, it was an easy call. This would be a great morning to catch up.

Mike found Henri chatting with another foursome at the first tee. Henri, gregarious as usual, used his short stature to literally look up at a conversation partner and draw out everything about his business. It was a gift, and Mike was convinced Henri used that French accent to his advantage by constantly asking open-ended questions. Mike only caught part of this conversation, but apparently the one with the nicely combed black hair called himself Frankie Urbino and he did something with email marketing.

"Henri, how's the weather in Brussels?" asked Mike as he approached the tee box.

"Cold, I expect," answered Henri.

Both men laughed.

Something about the men in Urbino's foursome seemed uncomfortable, so even though this group was scheduled to start after Mike and Henri's group, Mike was happy to let them tee off first.

Later, as they teed up for the par-5 tenth hole, Henri said, "Mike, may I discuss business for a few minutes?"

"Sure," said Mike. "Let's get our tee shots off and we can talk and walk."

The wives went first, hitting drives about 125 yards down the fairway. The men drove their tee shots about 100 yards further.

"Mike, you know I also sit on the Bullseye board," said Henri. "I know you and your bank worked with the FBI to help stop the flow of credit-card numbers from Bullseye to Russia and I am curious how you did it."

"We did more than that," said Mike. "We also sent those knuckleheads a message."

"Knucklehead? What is knucklehead?" asked Henri.

Mike laughed. "Always with the disarming French accent, Henri? You know perfectly well what a knucklehead is."

Henri also laughed. "You know me too well, my friend. What message did you send and how did you send it?"

"We told them they messed with the wrong bank," said Mike.

"Jesse Jonsen in our fraud department found a contractor who helped the FBI figure out how the credit-card numbers were flowing to Russia. We left it running for a couple extra days and substituted a few million expired and bogus credit-card numbers. We would have kept it up longer, but a blogger somehow got ahold of the story and we had to shut it down."

"How were you able to fool them?" asked Henri.

"That contractor made our fake data look the same as the real data. Jesse has all the details, but the guy posting the credit-card numbers up for sale disappeared a few days after posting some of our bogus numbers up for sale."

"I would like to talk to this contractor and to Jesse," said Henri. "Would that be okay?"

"Sure," said Mike. "I'll have Jesse call you and forward contact info for the contractor."

"Thank you," said Henri.

Mike and Henri would never find out how close they were to a key crook in the Bullseye breach.

The Boardroom

It was a typically cold late January morning in Minneapolis. It had dropped to double-digits below zero the night before, and the expected daytime high was -5. Nevertheless, the directors of Bullseye Corp. flew in from their balmier locations around the hemisphere to attend an emergency board meeting.

CEO Daniel Berger was on the defensive. He didn't want a board meeting. Why not wait until the next quarterly meeting in April? But Henri Carpentier, former chief operating officer with digital media powerhouse WooHoo Inc., led a faction overruling Berger. Carpentier sat on several boards and always talked about the security lessons he learned when somebody stole an American politician's email password while he was there. Berger thought Carpentier was a pain in the neck.

The Bullseye board of directors represented a who's who of business elite, including former and current Fortune 500 CEOs, media moguls, Internet entrepreneurs, financiers, and a former US Cabinet member. None of them wanted to experience January Minneapolis wind chills. But they were all painfully aware of recent federal regulations holding board members' feet to the fire, and recent headlines had made them willing to endure a few hours of cold to fight that fire.

Berger had faced angry boards before and he had a knack for making them see things his way. But with the latest quarterly statements and recent sensational headlines, this group would be tough. But they were nothing he couldn't handle. "A good crisis is where a great CEO shows his stuff, right?" he thought. "We have this data breach under control. The old divide-and-conquer approach will work with this bunch. I'll make the stockholders the enemy again. It's us against them. It's worked before. They'll come around." He looked over the room and took a breath. "Showtime."

He straightened up in his oversized executive chair, lowered his voice an octave, and addressed the group. "As we are all aware," Berger began, "we're here because a highly vocal group of shareholders want my head on a platter, and some of you are here to measure my head."

A few directors laughed. "That's good," he thought.

"I know we've been through a rough time with the Canada rollout and a disappointing recovery from the recession. I hoped the recent holiday season would break sales records. Instead, we were hit with the data breach. Fortunately, the news broke late enough in December that our holiday sales were only minimally impacted. It could have been much worse. On top of that we're facing a series of nuisance lawsuits from some shareholders and it could get expensive to make them go away.

"We need to look at that incident from the proper perspective," Berger continued. "We've all seen the headlines blaming us for the attack. And me, personally. And that's fine; I can take the heat. But the truth is, our success attracted a well-funded gang of greedy Russian super-hackers. They used sophisticated tactics on an unprecedented level to attack our great company. And, you know, there's something wrong when the press blames the victim for the crime. Make no mistake—we're the victims here. We need to educate our shareholders about that. The fact is, the press doesn't have the whole story. We did everything right and then some. You'll hear more about that in a minute."

"You're right, Mr. Berger," said Cameron Sandusky, board treasurer and former US secretary of agriculture. "From an economic perspective, this is just a blip on the screen. Sure, forty million sounds like a big number, but nobody was really affected that much. We weren't. Sales were a little shaky, but no shakier than the last few years. This whole episode is really nothing more than just an IT glitch."

Sandusky paused while he brushed a lock of his gray hair out of his eyes, looked up, and beamed a perfect smile.

"Are the rank-and-file shareholders really so concerned about a little technical problem? I don't think so. I'll bet they don't understand it, either. There are always a few troublemakers who become very loud in order to gain attention for themselves, but that doesn't mean we have to take it seriously. To be sure, fix any IT glitches we have. And then let's move on to a brighter tomorrow. Nobody will remember this story a year from now. And I'll take bets on that."

"Wise words indeed, Mr. Sandusky," said Berger, just as they had rehearsed. "Now, in order to give you more information about the data breach, we have two guests with us this morning. I don't need to introduce Liz Isaacs, our chief information officer. Most of you know her. I'm very proud of her leadership during the data breach. She called in the FBI and Uncle Sam Bank to quickly identify the leak—and confidentially, she devised a plot to send phony data back to the crooks and persuaded everyone else to go along with it. You saw my email last month, but I want to personally thank Liz for her leadership during this crisis."

He looked over at Liz, who was stunning in a navy Calvin Klein pantsuit. She gave an embarrassed nod, just as she'd practiced, and masked the worry behind her blue eyes. Why was this technician in the boardroom?

"Ordinarily, Liz's presence here would be sufficient to answer all your questions about the hacking and the leak and all those things, but apparently Mr. Carpentier thought differently. For reasons I cannot fathom, he invited a computer-service technician, Jerry Barkley. He's with the firm, Barkley IT. I gather it's a one-person firm. I'm sure you haven't heard of it. Nobody has. Mr. Barkley was along the evening our director of server operations, Ryan MacMillan, discovered the virus in our cash registers and directed the FBI toward the criminals in Russia. I personally gave Ryan a raise for that. Mr. Barkley—may I call you Jerry? I would like to thank you for keeping Ryan company that night. I think he said you bought some sandwiches or something? I'm sure that was a great help. As a gesture of our esteem for your services, please accept this twenty-five-dollar Bullseye gift card. Maybe it'll cover the cost of those sandwiches, huh?"

He held the gift card in the air for everyone to see before walking over and handing it to Jerry.

"Jerry, Jerry Barkley from Barkley IT, would you like to say a few words before you go?"

Jerry was stunned. Berger's account of the data breach sounded like it came from a parallel universe, a few million light-years from the actual truth here on Earth.

Once again, Jerry found himself to be the only person in the room not wearing a suit, but now he didn't care. As he looked at the gift card, he could feel a familiar low-level rage starting to boil in his belly. The same rage he'd felt last month when somebody tried to steal $10,000 from his business credit card. He took a deep breath and looked at Henri. Henri nodded in encouragement.

"Thanks, *Dan*. I'll try not to spend it all at once," said Jerry truthfully. "If you could validate my parking stub, we'll be all square."

Jerry turned to look at the former secretary of agriculture.

"Um, Cameron, right?"

"That's correct, Cameron *Sandusky*," he said, placing special emphasis on his last name.

"Well, *Cameron*," said Jerry, "with all due respect, this was more than just a little IT glitch. Forty million people's bank cards were compromised. That's not just a number on a balance sheet. Forty million *people* shopped at your store and for every single one of them, you helped some crook in Russia steal their credit-card number. And now bad guys around the world are using those numbers to steal from somebody else."

"No real harm done, no foul," said Cameron. "We all know the numbers. Yes, it was unfortunate, but the truth is, most of this was covered by insurance."

"You know what, Cameron?" said Jerry, his face becoming red. "There was plenty of harm and there were plenty of fouls in this whole thing. I was one of those forty million victims. Some clown tried to use my credit card to steal something like $10,000 worth of merchandise after I shopped here. I spent several hours of my life on the phone tracking it down and then several days of my life helping clean up your little mess. I guess that didn't show up on your spreadsheet. And multiply that by forty million other stories worse than mine. Did you see the little story buried inside the *Pioneer Press* the other day? After a welfare recipient in Wisconsin shopped at a Bullseye, somebody drained her cash card. She killed herself. Put that in your spreadsheet, *Cameron*."

"If you guys want to sweep it under the rug and forget about it, it's your company, so go right ahead. But I gotta tell ya, if that's what you want, I won't shop here again. I'm sure the little bit I spend isn't material on your financial statements. But forty million just like me, and forty million more of our friends? That adds up to a big number. So if you guys don't want to do something about this problem, then why am I here?"

"You are here," said Henri Carpentier, "because we value your perspective. As a native of Belgium, I have learned that to fully judge an issue, it is best to have more than one viewpoint. There is the American view, the Belgian view, the German view, and so forth. In this case you are an outside observer, yet you were involved in the investigation of our data breach. And according to my sources, you did much more than buy sandwiches for Ryan. So please, stay, my friend, and participate in our discussion. I look forward to hearing your views."

"But first," interrupted Berger, "let's hear from Liz Isaacs. I think she deserves a little round of applause."

Berger started clapping and most of the directors joined in, but not all of them. Liz stood and looked everyone in the eye, but then focused on Jerry.

"First," she began, "let me say I feel terrible about what happened to you, Jerry. On behalf of Bullseye I want to apologize to you and our forty million other guests for putting you through such an ordeal."

Now addressing the larger board, she continued, "This was a sophisticated attack from a ruthless group of overseas criminals. We worked extensively with the FBI to analyze what happened and we found this group attacked us with a series of incredibly complex hacking techniques. This wasn't some bored teenager, this was a well-funded criminal syndicate and they pulled out all the stops to come after us. But we've identified how they got in and we've plugged the holes. This won't happen again."

"So how did they get in?" asked Henri.

"They stole log-in credentials from a contractor and used those to exploit our network," said Liz. "And then they fooled all of us by using a video to steal our administrative credentials. From there, they planted malware on our point-of-sale terminals. The rest is history."

"How does one use a video to steal log-in credentials?" Henri asked.

"That was one of the most devious and brilliant components of this attack," said Liz. "They buried a new program in a video about website design that enabled them to log our activity."

Henri tried to loosen his tie, but the knot was too tight. "Are you telling us they planted a keylogger program in the computer of the CIO of this company?"

"As I said," said Liz, "this attack was like black magic. Through some miracle they planted this highly advanced program in my computer and in Ryan MacMillan's computer. It was remarkably clever and would have fooled Bill Gates, I'm sure."

"Wait a minute," said Jerry, "I can buy a keylogger program for something like fifty bucks. You guys sell them in your toy department. What's so sophisticated about their keylogger program? What, because it's Russian and sounds exotic?"

"It was a whole series of components," said Liz, "adding up to a multifaceted and brutal attack."

Henri finally loosened his tie so he could breathe, and looked across the table at Liz. "Not so, I am afraid. Forgive me, American English is not my native language, how do you say, our top IT people scratched the doggie?"

"I think the expression is, 'screwed the pooch,'" said Jerry. Looking at Liz, he said, "You fell for one of the oldest con jobs in the book."

"Yes," said Henri. "I am also curious, why did you not heed all the warnings and software notifications from your intrusion-detection systems?"

"I'm not a technician," said Liz, "but from what I understand, that system generated hundreds of false positives and our team missed those in a sea of false positive reports."

"The software was set up to notify a group email address," said Jerry. "So everyone in the group would get the notifications. But there was only one member of the group, and when she left the company last October, you got rid of her mailbox and didn't put anyone else in the group. So the notifications went into a black hole. Nobody saw them."

"Is this true?" asked Henri.

"I'm not a technician," said Liz. "I left those details to Ryan and his team."

Henri looked around the room. "Liz, Jerry, would you two step outside please? I would like to discuss some things privately with the board."

***

Plush was the only way to describe the lobby area outside the Bullseye boardroom. Liz sat down right away on one of the overstuffed chairs near the window and stared outside. The seating area was surrounded with low tables, each holding little bowls of Danish pretzels or mixed nuts. Jerry walked over to a larger table against the back wall filled with French pastries, fruit, yogurt, and coffee. A bucket of ice was well stocked with imported bottles of spring water and freshly squeezed juices. Artwork adorned the off-white walls, with track lights positioned in exactly the right spots to highlight the paintings. Underneath each painting was a little plaque with the name of the artist and a profile, along with a convenient pile of business cards with contact information.

"Nice touch," Jerry thought. "And a nice spread. I'm sure they won't miss an orange or two and a bottle of water." He walked around the room looking at the paintings while peeling an orange. It probably wouldn't violate any protocol to eat one of them—but was there a trash can for peelings? Yup, right next to one of those chairs and with a power outlet as a bonus.

He put down his backpack, pulled out a cell-phone charger, and plugged it in to the outlet, then laid his phone on the armrest and connected the phone to the charger. "Decent cell service," he thought as he looked at the signal strength of his cell phone. "The top floor does have its advantages." He broke his orange into sections and started to eat.

"I can't believe they're having this guy stick around!" thought Liz as she noticed a reflection of Jerry in the window. "Look at that bumpkin. He's obviously out of place here. His clothing is so tasteless and disrespectful. And when he contradicted me, I should have grabbed his geeky little neck and squeezed."

Jerry's cell phone rang. He wanted to answer but his fingers were sticky. He saw a stack of napkins on the snack table, but they were too far away. He quickly licked his fingers and poured a little Perrier on them, lifted up his pant legs, and wiped his fingers on his socks before grabbing the phone and answering it.

The ringing of the phone attracted Liz's attention.

"Hello, this is Jerry Barkley."

"Did he really just wipe his fingers on his… *white* socks?" Liz asked herself. "Where do they find Neanderthals like this? I think I'm going to be sick!"

"Oh, wow," said Jerry into his cell phone. "Um, yeah I can look at it from here. I'm in a meeting but we have a little break and I have my laptop with me. Do me a favor—give me about five minutes and I'll get right back to you…. Okay, groovy… Yup, I'll call you right back after I get set up."

Jerry ended the call and set the phone on the armrest. "Hey Liz, where's the bathroom?" he asked across the room.

"Huh?" said Liz. "Oh, you mean the restroom? Right down the hall, look on your left."

She wanted to tell him to go use the public library's facilities, six blocks away.

"Thanks," said Jerry, stuffing most of the rest of the orange in his mouth. "Sticky fingers."

Liz didn't say anything; she just stared back out the window, working to keep a neutral look on her face.

Jerry returned with his well-rinsed hands and opened his backpack. Liz glanced at him, disappointed that he hadn't gotten lost. "Curious," she thought. His backpack has a logo with a graphic of a white face wearing a red Fedora hat. The words "red hat" in lowercase letters were next to the figure of the face wearing the hat. She couldn't help but ask, "What's with the red hat?"

Jerry looked up from his laptop. "Red Hat is an open-source software company. You haven't heard of them?"

"We don't bother with open-source companies. We can't afford any mistakes, so we only use reputable companies."

"Uh-huh," said Jerry as he finished setting up his laptop and portable Wi-Fi hotspot. "You might want to look into some of the open-source initiatives out there. Some of those could have helped you back in December." To himself, Jerry thought, "With that kind of attitude, it's no wonder these guys lost forty million credit-card numbers."

"What *are* you doing?" asked Liz.

"I have a customer with a branch office that's half offline. Twenty people can't work," said Jerry. "It's costing them a fortune every second."

"Half offline?" asked Liz.

"Yeah. And I know why. My automation sent out an email on it a few minutes ago. I'm doing backup routing at this site and the offline stuff is probably trying to route directly through their MPLS circuit instead of using me as a gateway. Which pretty much defeats the purpose."

"Okay," said Liz, clueless.

"I watch their primary telecom connection back to the headquarters office," said Jerry, trying to explain. "If I see a problem, I change the routing to go through a backup tunnel using the Internet. And then when the primary telecom connection's okay again, I put the

The Boardroom

routing back. It's kind of like if I-94 between Minneapolis and St. Paul is messed up, redirect everyone to use University Avenue instead. The whole thing's automated and it's pretty slick. But it only works if they use my stuff as a gateway. They have to ask me which path to follow."

Jerry pulled out a small case from his pocket. He opened it, took out some portable reading glasses, and put them on.

Jerry noticed Liz watching him. "You can do depth or detail, but not both anymore," he chuckled. "I forgot I had fingerprints until I started wearing these. I still look at my fingers through these things—they're amazing!"

"Idiot!" thought Liz, as she watched Jerry type commands and finger the touchpad. A few seconds later, Jerry picked up his cell phone and dialed a number.

"Hey, Dean, it's Jerry. Here's what you need to do. On every dead device, change the default gateway from dot 100 to dot 254. Yup, that's right. Dot 100 is the IP address for the MPLS router. And dot 254 is my stuff. You have to route through me and then I'll either take you through the primary path or the backup path. But if you don't route through me, you're stuck on the primary path and when it's down, so are you... Yeah, I know for a fact your MPLS is down... Because my stuff noticed it and sent out an automated email... Okay, test me. Change the gateway on one dead PC and see if it comes back alive... Yeah, I can talk you through that... Well, you've got nothing to lose. It's dead in the water right now, right?... So if it doesn't work, put it back the way it was... Yeah, this will work. And find the make and model of your IP phones and I'll see if I can find some documentation on how to change those."

Liz listened as Jerry spoke another language resembling English on the phone.

After a few minutes of gibberish, she heard, "Of course it worked… Thanks, but I get scared when people call me a genius. It's not genius, it's testing. Now, on your phones, I found a PDF with some instructions and I'm sending it to you."

After a few more minutes, Liz heard Jerry say, "You're welcome… No, just keep routing through me and then I'll make the decision on how to send it out… No, don't change it back, keep it the way it is… Groovy. Talk to ya later."

"Well, that was intense," said Jerry to no one in particular, rubbing his ear after the long conversation. "And a great example of open source in action."

"How's that?" asked Liz.

"These guys have a first-class automated backup routing system and they paid something like twenty cents on the dollar for it versus the proprietary stuff," said Jerry.

"Didn't you just spend a half hour with them on the phone making it work?" asked Liz.

"No, I spent a half hour teaching them to use it," said Jerry. "If they'd done what I told them to do in the first place, we wouldn't have had to go through this. My stuff did its job."

"May as well take care of some emails as long as I have all this out," said Jerry.

Sounds of muffled voices occasionally came through the boardroom walls, but the words were impossible to decipher. The tone seemed angry and Liz and Jerry could hear raised voices, followed by quieter discussions.

"I wonder what's the big deal in there," said Jerry, although had a pretty good idea.

"I wouldn't know," lied Liz. She stared off into space while Jerry continued with email.

The Boardroom

After a few minutes Ryan MacMillan walked into the room. He saw Liz, staring off into space, trying to look composed and Jerry doing something on his laptop.

Jerry looked up. "Hey, Ryan—you're looking healthy."

"Yeah, um, you too," said Ryan.

"What are you doing here, Ryan?" asked Liz. "Is the board having an open house?"

"They just called me and asked me to come up right away," said Ryan. "I'm supposed to knock on the door."

Ryan knocked, and a few seconds later Henri Carpentier opened the door. "Ah, Ryan, very good. Liz, would you also join us please? Jerry, please indulge us for a few more minutes. Feel free to find something to eat."

Jerry watched as Henri escorted Liz and Ryan into the boardroom. The board members all looked down or away as Liz and Ryan took seats and Henri closed the door.

Five minutes later, the door flew open and Liz stormed from the boardroom, followed by Ryan a few feet behind her. They quickly walked through the lobby, out the main door and down the hall. Jerry heard fading footsteps, and then silence followed by the ding of the elevator as it arrived to carry them away.

"Wow," thought Jerry. "I should probably put my laptop away." Suddenly self-conscious, he pulled his pant legs down as far as he could to cover his white socks and then began packing up his laptop and portable hotspot. "They can't fire me," Jerry smiled. "I don't work here!"

Shortly after that, the elevator dinged again. Jerry heard more footsteps approaching.

"Are they sending security guards after me?" he thought. He quickly grabbed another orange from the snack table and stuffed it into his backpack. He zipped it up completely.

After a few seconds, the person responsible for the footsteps came in. She had long, graying hair wrapped into a bun on top of her head. She wore a knee-length skirt. She walked straight to the boardroom door without even acknowledging Jerry.

She knocked briefly and handed an envelope to Henri when he answered. "Merci, Brittany," he said.

"You're welcome," she said. The door closed and Jerry watched her walk briskly through the lobby and down the hall. She never acknowledged Jerry, as if he didn't exist.

"Get a grip, Jerry. You get paid to be paranoid, but this is ridiculous."

The door to the boardroom opened again and this time Henri beckoned Jerry in. Jerry picked up his backpack and followed Henri into the room. A sea of eyes focused on him as he moved through the door.

Before Jerry could sit down, Henri said, "Jerry, first, I would like to thank you on behalf of the entire board for spending your time with us. We are all businesspeople and we know how valuable your time is. Please accept this check for $1,500 from Bullseye for your consulting time today," as he handed the envelope to Jerry. "And now, how do you say, may we poke your brain?"

"Pick your brain," corrected one of the board members. Everyone in the room laughed easily, except for Cameron and Berger.

"Um, wow, thanks!" said Jerry. He was dumbfounded. Maybe this group wasn't so bad after all.

"We know $1,500 is small compensation for this day of your time," said Henri. "But please indulge us with our questions."

"Sure, pick away," said Jerry, recovering from the pleasant surprise and regretting his choice of socks even more. He found an empty chair, placed his backpack under the table, muted his cell phone, and sat down.

"Very well," said Henri. "What steps could an organization such as ours take to fend off such attacks in the future?"

"Well, first some tactical stuff," said Jerry. "Topology counts. Segregate your network and protect those POS terminals. Put them behind their own firewall. They should only interact with a small set of IP addresses and you can log and drop any interactions with anything else."

Jerry looked around the room. "Since we're all businesspeople, I guess you'll appreciate my shameless plug. I can build you some firewalls that'll do the job nicely." A few board members laughed approvingly. Cameron and Berger stayed silent.

"And while you're at it, also logically and physically isolate the systems your outside contractors use. You have a bazillion contractors—what are the odds at least one of them will have their password into your network compromised? Pretty good, right? So why do your contractors have visibility into the most sensitive parts of your network? Think about this—the Russians stole log-in credentials into a payment system from a contractor and used that to recon your entire network. That's nuts!

"Diligence also counts. You guys spent millions of dollars for a system to watch over your network and then farmed it all out to India. And then you didn't pay any attention when your group in India tried to warn you. What's up with that?"

"And that was a major reason we just released our CIO and her direct report," said Berger. "It's obvious to me now our IT resources didn't have a grasp on the importance of security. We're now looking for new resources who will be more diligent, as you say. And that's why we authorized spending millions more dollars to accelerate the chip and PIN program. In the next few months, we'll have chip-enabled cards in everyone's hands and terminals to read them. We'll lead the industry."

Jerry laughed out loud. "That's kind of like putting new tires on the car to fix a broken engine. Good to do, but it doesn't solve the problem. And just for the record, I'm not a resource, I'm a person."

"So beyond the chip and PIN investment, now you want me to spend even more money on tech toys?" asked Berger. "In case you hadn't noticed, we're not a tech company, we're a retailer."

"I guess that all depends on how badly you want to fix your problem," said Jerry. "I'm sure your PR people can put out some nice news releases about new credit cards with chips. Do you want to solve the problem or just spend money doing PR?"

"That's a loaded question," said Berger, "and I resent it."

"And that brings up a fundamental issue," said Jerry. "Your attitude needs an overhaul. You can spend a lot of money retrofitting and take false comfort believing you're secure. But the truth is, security needs to be at the core of all your operations, not a bolted-on afterthought.

"And Dan, I have an exercise for you," said Jerry, holding out his arms. "How many arms do I have?"

"Okay, two," said Berger, looking perplexed.

"And how many legs?" asked Jerry.

"This is silly," said Berger.

"Yes, it is," said Jerry. "Because you and I have the same number of arms and legs and we probably both put our pants on one leg at a time, why am I a resource and you're a full-fledged person?"

"This is ridiculous," said Cameron. "Why is this technician lecturing us?"

"Because somebody stole forty million credit cards from you and your customers," answered Jerry. "And if you don't learn the right lessons from this experience, they'll be back for more. You're already the board of directors in charge of the biggest credit-card theft in history. Want to be part of the next one?"

"Think about it this way," continued Jerry. "You know how all the business textbooks tell you good marketing is key to good sales? Well, they should also tell you that good security is key to good operations. You don't outsource it offshore, you don't buy it from a software store, you integrate it with everything you do.

"And Cameron, if you think the tech stuff is only tangential for day-to-day running of the company, you're shortsighted," continued Jerry. "Information is at the heart of everything you do. Without information, you don't have sales. Your information is the most valuable asset you have. You need somebody to focus on making sure everything in the company, from top to bottom, takes into account the confidentiality, integrity, and availability of your information."

"This sounds like a big mountain to climb," said Henri.

"It is," said Jerry. "If it were easy, everyone would be doing it."

"And now I have another question," asked Henri. "Is IT a core function of the business or just another service like building maintenance or corporate travel?"

"I'm an IT guy, so you already know how I'll answer that question," said Jerry. "But let me ask a question in return. How many of you do anything differently today than you did, say, five years ago?"

Jerry waited a few seconds but nobody responded.

"Oh, really!" he said. "So you're telling me you none of you do anything different today than you did in 2008?"

"Not me," mocked Cameron.

"Okay," said Jerry. "Let's try this a different way. How do you use your cell phones?"

"Um, we talk on them," said a board member. Others laughed.

"Yeah, I get that a lot," said Jerry. "How many of you text on your cell phones? How many check websites on your phones and compare prices when you're shopping? How many use your cell phones for email? How many use tablets to read books?"

Most of the room nodded. "That's what I thought," said Jerry. "How many of you back up your pictures and videos at home to somewhere in the cloud? For that matter, how many use your cell phones these days to take pictures and video?"

"Yeah, so what?" asked another board member.

"So here's the point," said Jerry. "How many of you did those things back in 2008?"

All the board members looked at each other. Most shrugged their shoulders. "You know as well as me that none of you did any of that stuff back in 2008. A lot of what we do routinely today was science fiction back then—just five years ago."

"So now," continued Jerry, "what do you think drives these innovations?"

"Money," said Berger. "Somebody wanted to make money so they invented these things."

"Yup," said Jerry. "So if somebody is making money, what does that mean?"

Nobody answered.

"And you guys are the smartest businesspeople on the planet?" asked Jerry. "If somebody is making money, then somebody else is spending money, right? We're all spending lots of money on new technology to collect and analyze *information* and move it around this planet. IT innovations are all around you, and they're behind all the new stuff you've done over the past five years. IT is behind that loyalty card program you guys put together. And IT will be behind new stuff five years from now we can't even imagine today."

"So, Henri, to answer your question," said Jerry, "IT is at the center of everything we do these days, even with companies you would think are far away from anything IT related."

"Great speech," said Cameron. "Got me right in the gut. Really, I have tears swelling in my eyes."

"So now, what," asked Berger, "we put IT resources in charge of all the technology?"

"I told you before," said Jerry. "I'm a person, not a resource. And yeah, you put IT professionals in charge of IT."

"And we'll end up with a company full of elegant technology that has no benefit," said Berger. "Not while I'm in charge."

"You put a marketing person in charge of IT before," said Jerry. "How did that work out for you? Look—in what other profession is subject-matter expertise a liability instead of an asset? Would you put, say, a plumber in charge of the finance department? Would you put an engineer in charge of sales? So why do you put people who know nothing about IT in charge of the IT department?"

"Because we need leaders and not technicians in charge of that department," said Berger. "And IT people are technicians, not leaders."

"And with that attitude leading this company," said Jerry, "somebody will come along and take all your customers away. And that's after somebody else comes along and steals some more secrets from you."

Turning to Henri, Jerry said, "Henri and everyone, thanks for asking me to come in today. And thanks for the check. Really—this is a lot more meaningful than a firm handshake. Unless you have any more questions, it's probably time for me to go."

"Let us take a short break," said Henri to the directors, "while I walk Jerry to the elevator."

Once they were out of earshot, Henri offered some advice to Jerry.

"Do not let the members of this group, how do I say, get in your skin."

"Get under my skin?" asked Jerry.

"Yes," said Henri. "American English has so much slang. Your ideas have more support on this board than you think. And there are other issues unrelated to IT. Do not be surprised if I call upon you again, perhaps about forming some sort of longer-term arrangement."

"I'll look forward to hearing from you, Henri," said Jerry as he pressed the elevator button.

"And one more thing, Jerry. Here's a parking voucher for our ramp."

Jerry smiled. The elevator dinged and he walked inside.

"Merci beaucoup, Henri!"

"Take care, Jerry. Au revoir."

The elevator closed and Jerry rode down. As usual, he forgot where he parked in the parking ramp and it took him nearly twenty minutes to find his car.

***

Two months later, Jerry noticed a news item on the front page of the business section as he ate his lunch of almost raw hamburger and microwaved green beans.

The headline read, "Daniel Berger steps down as CEO, board chairman for Bullseye."

"It looks like they're done with that resource," thought Jerry. "A fitting end."

Acknowledgments

Until now, I never paid attention to acknowledgments. That's because I'm a rookie author who had no clue what it takes to create a usable manuscript and then turn it into a real book that (hopefully) somebody will want to buy. I gotta tell ya, it's a huge project and the author is just one member of a larger team. I need to thank a bunch of people, so please read through just a few more pages while I acknowledge the members of this team. If you enjoyed this book—especially if you took away some lessons—thank them with me because this team turned rough raw material into a story that held your interest.

First, of course is family. I started the original manuscript in January 2014 and turned in the first draft that October. I worked on much of it between midnight and 5:00 a.m, or over weekends when I neglected countless house and grandpa duties. My wife, Tina, says she missed me in bed. Well, I missed her too. Thanks, Tina, for loaning me to this project. If this book is successful, maybe we'll splurge on a vacation to someplace exotic, maybe an overnight trip to a hotel in Duluth, Minnesota.

Next up is Lily Coyle, with Beaver's Pond Press. I met Lily for the first time in September 2013, when I gave her some material to look over. When she asked what genre I was writing, I didn't know what a genre was. Since the material was a bunch of essays about how I grew up, we decided it was a memoir. She looked it over and told me

Acknowledgments

I needed to learn how to tell a story. She recommended a bunch of books about editing and storytelling. I read them all, cover to cover, and tried to apply what I learned before I came back thirteen months later with my first draft of this story.

Steve LeBeau did the content editing. Steve says content editing is a destructive process, where the editor tears apart the author's hard work and helps build it back better and stronger. Steve took a 94,000-word manuscript and chopped it to smithereens, leaving a tighter 60,000-word manuscript. Steve taught me that stories have protagonists for a reason and he wrote the first draft of the "Cybercrime Seminar" chapter to introduce the characters in this story. Yup, that's right—my name is on the front cover as the author, but Steve wrote the first draft of that first chapter. Steve also had the idea for the last chapter, where Jerry Barkley finds himself in front of the Bullseye Stores board of directors and dishes out advice. I wrote that chapter, but it was Steve's idea to put it in. Steve's work is all over the story as he refined many of my rough ideas into something workable and threw out the lousy ideas. I think Steve's name should also be on the front cover, but Steve asked me to acknowledge him here, instead. So thanks, Steve—a good chunk of this story is yours.

Speaking of editing, I'm an IT tech guy, which means IT details are my friend. This is a double-edged sword. When I'm tracking down a security issue in real life, you want me on top of every detail. But when writing a fiction story, many of those details are torture for readers. Lily Coyle to the rescue. I was struggling with how much detail to put in a tough passage of the story, where the Russians were performing reconnaissance on the Bullseye network. I sent an 813-word sample to Lily and asked for some advice. After telling me I put her to sleep three times, she sent me back 485 words a couple hours later that told exactly what I wanted to tell, with enough detail to make sense, but not so much that it was overpowering. I used what she gave me, word for word. It was a breakthrough moment. Thanks, Lily.

And speaking of details, Alicia Ester is amazing. She wrote an entire style guide tailored for this book. I'm struggling to apply it right now. I took a couple of English classes in college. I figured that gave me a working knowledge of English grammar. Thanks to Alicia, the world will still believe that myth. But now I know better. Alicia, thanks for saving me from myself.

I don't know how editors do it; it's a gift.

Cover design and page layout—wow, who knew all the work that goes into that! Laura Drew did the book cover. Laura is an artist and a pro. I have no clue how she comes up with her designs—it's another gift. She gave me four great-looking designs to choose from. So then I tried an experiment, designing an additional book cover sample based on a picture of a POS system in a store. "Bad" is too polite a word for what I came up with.

Page layout is another can of worms and Laura's work is on every single page of this book. Reproducing output from emails, chat logs, and computer commands that normally displays on a video monitor is not easy to do on a printed page. Laura, thanks for making both the inside and outside of this book look great.

And thanks to the whole publishing team for patiently educating a rookie author.

A few friends read through some early drafts and gave me feedback. Fredy saved me from an embarrassing issue with money. Jeff said, "You need to grab me!" Don was more polite, when he said, "Greg, I'm, um, well, I'm not an IT guy." That feedback helped make this a better story. Don agreed to read a later draft, probably against his better judgment, after Steve and I fixed the opening chapters. Don ended up liking it and that feedback helped keep me moving forward, especially after his candid appraisal early on. Seriously, if a friend asks you to read an early draft of a manuscript, give the author honest feedback and don't sugarcoat it. It's the best favor you can do. Fredy, Jeff, and Don, I owe you an autographed copy of this book.

Acknowledgments

Finally, and mostly, thank you, the reader, for taking a chance on a rookie author and spending your money and time to read this whole story. If you like what you read, would you do me a favor and write a glowing, five-star online review? That will help others find this book and help the project pay for itself. And if this project supports itself financially, I'll write another book and maybe another one after that. I enjoy the process.

By now, the best editors and designer in the business have gone over this story, line by line. But I had final approval over everything, which means I own all the mistakes, typos, inconsistencies, or other problems. If you find a problem, contact me via Beaver's Pond Press and let me know about it so we can fix it for the next edition. If you're the first to find the problem, I'll make sure you get an autographed copy of the book with my thanks.

Greg Scott, March 15, 2015